MICK MACNEIL

Spooked

Contents

1	Chap. 1. Eyeopener	1
2	Chap 2 Bad Kool Aid	8
3	Chap. 3. Grave Situation	12
4	Chap. 4. Do Ya Ken Done In	14
5	Chap. 5. If the Grave Fitz	18
6	Chap. 6. No Scratches Please	21
7	Chap. 7. Put It to Rest	25
8	Chap. 8. Steeling Away	30
9	Chap. 9. Steel Back	33
10	Chap. 10. The Skinny on Nick	37
11	Chap. 11. Lost Ground	42
12	Chap. 12. Seekers Finders	48
13	Chap. 13. Murder He Said	53
14	Chap. 14. Kwick	57
15	Chap. 15. Ally	62
16	Chap. 16. But You're Dead	67
17	Chap. 17. Get Him	72
18	Chap. 18. The Story	76
19	Chap. 19. Catching a Killer	78
20	Chap. 20. Found a Friend	82
21	Chap. 21. Investigations	87
22	Chap. 22. Dead Reckoning	92
23	Chap. 23. Evil Dead	96
24	Chap. 24. Kwick Again	100

25	Chap. 25. We Got Trouble	105
26	Chap. 26. See That	110
27	Chap. 27, Yeah, Thanks Doc	114
28	Chap. 28, Add D to Evil	119
29	Chap. 29. Being the Target	124
30	Chap. 30. Tracking Evil	128
31	Chap. 31. Chivot	132
32	Chap. 32. Rickert Again	137
33	Chap. 33. Paranormal Investigators	142
34	Chap. 34. Rickert's Arsonist	147
35	Chap. 35. Spirit Zappers	152
36	Chap. 36. Meet Fitz	157
37	Chap. 37. A Weird Aura	162
38	Chap. 38. Team Building	166
39	Chap. 39. Fly in the Ointment	172
40	Chap. 40. Lost and Found	177
41	Chap. 41. Goodbye and Good Luck	182
42	Chap. 42 New Structure	187
43	Chap. 43. Ready to Burn	192
44	Chap. 44. Battle and Wakening	197
45	Chap. 45. Aftermath	202
46	Chap. 46. The Phone Rang	207

1

Chap. 1. Eyeopener

Ghosts! Don't talk to me about ghosts. I don't want to hear your theories about lingering emotional stress, electromagnetic interference, toxic mold, unfinished business or the afterlife. For most of my life, ghosts were things found on TV shows and in movies. They were fantastical, scary, and unreal. When the lights went up and the doors opened, the last bit, unreal, was all that remained. I liked it that way. So, unless we are sitting around a campfire listening to spooky stories, I don't want to hear about ghosts.

I prefer the world of ordinary because for years, that was my life, ordinary, work, play, repeat, nothing special, and while not particularly rousing, it was good enough for Mr. nondescript, me.

Five times a week, sometimes more, I took that old commuter train into the city, usually mornings and back to my small town home in the evenings. I didn't mind the commuter ride to work each day. On the way to the city, I could sleep, and on the way home I could plan my evenings. Well. That usually took about from the time I first sat down until the train left the station. The rest of the time, I was in some other space, but like I said, it didn't bother me.

I had a reasonably decent job; the pay was good, and the workload wasn't too stressful. I liked the job, and I liked the city, but home was the small town an hour and a half away. It was a great little town. I had grown up there, went to school there, had my first love there, then we went to high school and that ended, but so what. I had some good friends, friends I had met while at school and on various sports teams. Over the years, the love of sports had evolved from participation to primarily team support at the local watering hole on game day.

We still played a bit, slow pitch in the summer, touch football in the fall and pickup hockey during the winter. Most of the time, it was just hanging out after work, at a buddy's house or the local drinking, and eating establishment, Roadside Sports Bar. For the chief part, it was work and that daily train ride there and back.

Like I said, most mornings I dozed my way to the city stop where I got off and walked the block to work. In the evening, it was the same trip only in reverse, most of the time I spent staring off into space with a few minutes focused on the daily news.

That had gone for nearly two years. Then one day between the station and the office, I came across a storefront shop I can't remember ever having seen before. The name on the door said Kwick Optometry. The signs in the window promised cheap prices and better vision.

I had broken the nose piece on my glasses, trying to slide into second under a tag. The glasses still worked but had an annoying tilt. I couldn't remember ever having seen this shop before, although I must have passed it every day. I figured I hadn't noticed it because until now; I didn't need it.

There it was, so I stepped in to see if I could get my glasses repaired. There was a small counter, with some eye glass frames and a box of loose eyeglass parts. Nothing else seemed to be there except for one shelf with a very limited and, to my mind, hideous looking collection of glasses. A nondescript lady with straight, greyish blonde hair, excessive eye shadow and bright red lips, wearing a gray cardigan with the emblem of some university or college I'd never heard of, stood behind the counter. She asked if she could help me, and I explained my issue. Then she added, "Certainly we can help, but you'll need to see the optometrist first."

I felt it an unnecessary imposition, especially as I was running a little late for work, so I asked, "Is it really necessary just to get glasses fixed?"

"Oh yes," she replied. "Doc Dabra has to see all our customers. It will only take a minute."

She ushered me into a small room. It was empty except for a threadbare patient chair and a couple of pieces of equipment. It looked nearly as ancient as the gentleman, with the white hair and shaggy mustache that matched the white coat he wore, standing beside the chair. It looked something like a dentist's chair. Similar to everything else in the shop, including the old guy, it looked ancient and well used. The old fellow, obviously Dr. Dabra, pointed to the chair. "Take a seat, young man," he said.

I explained about the glasses. He leaned close and in a quiet, even voice said, "Son, forget the glasses. In two minutes, I can have you seeing better than you ever have."

I was about to demur when he swung something that looked like an old pair of binoculars on a rotating stand toward me.

"Take a look in there," he said, and for some reason, I did.

I could see nothing, and I told him so. "Oh, you will," he said, and clicked something on the binoculars and moved them away.

"There," he said.

Then he took the glasses I was holding from my hand and tossed them into the garbage pail beside the chair. "Won't need those anymore."

To be honest, I had no idea what he was talking about and reached into the garbage to retrieve my glasses when I realized I could see perfectly without them. He was right; I didn't need them anymore. Then he asked for my insurance and wrote down the information from my card on what looked like a scrap of newspaper. "Don't worry," he said with an odd looking smile, "Let me deal with that, and," he held the piece of newspaper up to his eye, "as for you Mr. Bannon, enjoy your glasses free life and," after a pause, he added, "believe me your vision is now far better than you ever dreamed possible."

Strangely enough, as I walked out the door without glasses, something I had worn most of my life, the last few minutes slipped away. I kept only a vague memory of Kwick Optometry, and no one who knew me seemed to even notice I was no longer wearing my glasses. When I pointed it out to my friends at the pub after the next game, most shrugged. One who was a bit sharper than the others said. "It's no big deal, I had laser vision correction too."

I didn't remember any laser. In fact, I remembered only vaguely about glasses and optometry. Perhaps that was why I never again saw the Kwick Optometry shop on my walks to and from the station. I know now but getting there is a long story. I'll get to it.

As I said, I'd been riding that train for around two years,

doing the same thing day after day, morning, doze, afternoon, gaze. But shortly after my vaguely remembered visit to Kwick Optometry, where I thought I might have gotten laser vision correction, something changed. I was on my way home when the coach wheels must have squealed or something as we took a corner. It brought me to full consciousness, and I found myself looking out the window at what had to be a derelict house. The place was in disrepair, windows broken, roofing torn, shingles missing, side view of a bleached wood porch. A dirty and cracked window, probably a kitchen window on the main floor, caught my attention.

After that, I continued to doze my way to the city in the mornings, but on the homeward bound run, I looked for that derelict house. Like clockwork, the train would take that slight bend to the right and there it would be, the ruin of a house in all its disrepair. And that window, too dirty to reflect back any of the evening light. I couldn't help myself. I had to look. It called to me.

So now my commuter ride home had incorporated a routine, and, unbelievably, it was one I never missed. Over time, I could see the house continue to fall deeper into disrepair. After watching the house and the window day after day for several months, it surprised me one evening to see what looked like a cat on the inside ledge of the window. What's more, the window seemed clear and uncracked. I really thought little about it. Likely a stray had found its way in and climbed up on the ledge, the sight of it so distracting me I hadn't really noticed the dirt and the cracks I had been looking at for months.

The next day, the window was back to normal, no cat behind it, dirty and cracked as usual. It stayed that way for several weeks before I saw the cat in the window again. It seemed to show up more frequently as the days passed until eventually it was there every day. I didn't know why, but I felt there was something strange about the cat. Why I thought that, I wasn't sure. From what I could make out as the train zipped past, it was a pretty ordinary tan-furred cat.

About that time, with the first stirrings of fall, my slo-pitch team would end its season by heading south for a tournament. Our team was good enough to last most of the week. Several of us would take a second week, get in some golf, and bask in the warmth that had already left our hometown behind. After two weeks, it was back to sweater weather and on the first morning back to work; I dozed on that train. I nearly missed my stop and had to push back the doors as I jumped out.

It was a long first day back at work and boarding the commuter train; I was pretty tired. I barely made it to my favorite window seat when I dozed off.

I've always found the motion and the sound of the train relaxing. This time, I did more than relax. I napped. Neither fully asleep nor awake, I opened my eyes just as the old house came into view. I blinked my eyes and upon opening them, the car I was in had nearly passed the house, but I thought I saw a face in the window looking over the cat in my direction. I couldn't be sure, having only caught a glimpse as the train quickly left the old house behind.

My onboard routine normalized, and I watched for the old house more carefully. I saw the cat in the window, but no sign of anything or anyone else. Then it happened again, a week later. I'm sure I saw someone in the window looking out at the train. It didn't happen every day, but often, I would see the face looking out the window over the cat watching the train go by.

The face, I could tell, belonged to that of an older teenage or

6

young adult. She had a lovely face framed by light colored hair. I couldn't tell much beyond that as the house was a distance from the track and the train passed very quickly.

I wondered who this person, it looked like a girl, in the window was. Had someone bought the place and moved in while I was on holidays. I could see no changes to the building, and I doubted it was very habitable as it was. Perhaps she was homeless and had moved in for the winter, or perhaps she was a member of a homeless gang or group, probably crackheads who hid out in the house.

I have to admit, none of this made much sense. The house was a complete wreck and since I had begun my daily watch, had grown more dilapidated. There had to be far better places out there, even for druggies or homeless kids. My curiosity was aroused, and I would have to take a look.

2

Chap 2 Bad Kool Aid

You might assume it would be easy to find a place along a little over an hour long express run. You would be wrong. It took three days of scanning google maps, satellite views and some old county maps in the local library. According to documents that were with the township maps, the house with the face in the window was on part of a large tract of land owned collectively by a communal group calling themselves the New Structure. They purchased the land around the end of the second world war. There were four separate farms, including barns and houses on the commune. The community was successful over the second half of the century, but then was suddenly disbanded around nineteen ninety

I was intrigued by the whole thing, a communal collective prosperous for thirty years, suddenly falling apart almost overnight. As it turned out, somewhere in the late sixties, a son of one of the original founders assumed leadership of the commune. He fancied himself to be more than just a community leader. He decided for reasons of his own he was the one chosen to be a spiritual leader as well. As time passed, he became more of a cult leader than a collective leader.

It was around this time some youthful members of the collective disappeared. The local constabulary, although suspicious, had little regard for Carl Chivot, the self-proclaimed cult guru. They believed those who had disappeared had taken off from the collective to find a better, less controlled life elsewhere.

Mostly, it was true. The police continued a half-hearted investigation as more and more runaways from the cult showed up, living well away from the place. The investigation, while still officially under way, pretty much faded. It remained on the books as 'ongoing.' In the field, it was all but done.

The stress of it all must have affected Chivot. He became paranoid and eventually emotionally disturbed enough to think the ongoing investigation was a message from God telling him to liberate his followers. He believed God had given him the key to the back door of heaven and a Jonesville style ending would bring them all there. He called the community together, promised them a passage into heaven, and gave them all a glass of specially prepared "Kool-Aid" to drink after a fortunately long and involved prayer session. I say fortunately because while he was turned to face the giant cross on the back wall of the meeting room, many community members snuck out. Those who remained poured their drinks onto the earthen floor so that when the time came to down the drink and step through heaven's back door, the only one with a full glass was Chivot himself.

While the others feigned drinking, he downed the "prepared Kool-Aid" which, by the way, was not "Kool Aid." The drink was actually a bad tasting cider Chivot had brewed from rotten apples the week before and laced with heaven knows what.

As Chivot collapsed to the floor in death, those remaining

9

headed off, leaving his body behind for the police investigation. The police declared Chivot's suicide a death by misadventure and closed the case shortly after. By then, the collective was deserted. The houses, left empty, although of particularly sturdy construction, were given over to the forces of nature and their ultimate destruction.

Armed with that bit of information, for what it was worth, and a map, I decided to pay a visit and find out who had taken over the derelict home. After a half hour run from home and another thirty minutes on badly kept gravel roads, I came to the house. It looked as dilapidated from this vantage point as it had from the train window.

The driveway was so badly overgrown and with so many hidden washouts; it forced me to leave my car on the road and began on foot to make my way cautiously towards the house. Turning back, I noticed a bearded man in a long robe leaning against a fence post across the road, looking at me. I waved, but he made no response.

The driveway was perilous. On two occasions, I came close to twisting an ankle. The porch stoop of the house was no less dangerous. It and the floor of the porch beyond it were rotted and broken. I carefully made my way to the door, stepping from what appeared to be one of the driest and sturdiest looking boards to another. The screen door was slightly ajar and the main door beyond it wide open. Given the look of the floor, it had been that way for a long time.

I stepped through the doorway into the house. The overwhelming odor of mildew and rot filled the air, making my eyes water. As I came to the kitchen door, I could see the girl from the window, her back to me as she seemed intent on food preparation. I was about to comment on the unsanitary nature of the prep area when she shouted, "where have you been? You're late, mom's away, and Carl wants to come over later."

Then she turned to face me. I don't care how many zombies, crime forensics or horror shows you've seen, nothing prepares you for the sight of someone's hideously decomposed face. Especially when it's talking to you. I made a rather unmanly shriek and, turning, took off for the door. I was moving so fast that I seemed to glide over the deteriorated floorboards and down the driveway to my car. I didn't step anyone place on the deck and down the road long enough to fall victim to a rotted piece of board or washout and was in my car in seconds.

Without looking back, I made a U turn, just barely avoiding the damp, muddy ditches that lined both sides of the road and took off for home. I can't say for certain, but I think the guy with the beard and robe leaning against a fence-post was laughing at me. I didn't look back to confirm.

I was a mess for the rest of the weekend. During the day, I couldn't get the vision of the decomposing face out of my head. When at night I finally got to sleep, it was filled with nightmares. On the way back to work Monday morning, I did something that I had never done for nearly five years. I sat on the other side of the coach. I had no desire to see that house again, even out of the corner of my eye. From then on, I made it a point to sit on the other side of the train away from the windows that looked out on the house.

3

Chap. 3. Grave Situation

I spent the next few weeks trying to avoid thinking about the house and the horrific vision. Eventually, I was able to convince myself it was only a trick of the light on piles of refuse blown in through open windows and doors. For most of that time, I buried my nose in one of those free newspapers you can pick up at commuter stations; not that I read more than a word or two.

As the passing weeks slowly erased my memory of the house and what I might have seen there, I would let the paper slip onto my lap. My glance occasionally went to the window, but I paid scant attention to the dreary surroundings passing by. I don't know what drew my attention to the big cemetery spread out beyond the window, close to my city stop.

I may not have paid any attention to much out the window, but for some reason, I noticed that cemetery. I didn't detect the man in the suit when he first showed up to stand at the cemetery fence and watch the train pass. After I did, he was there at the same time, standing faithfully beside the fence.

He was pretty well dressed to be a cemetery worker. He

looked to me like someone who came into the cemetery for a few minutes' peace before heading to work or going home. Morning and evening, he was there. Just standing, observing the train go by. After seeing him there every day for several weeks, it surprised me one afternoon to see him wave at the train. It was just a reflex, but I waved back as if his wave was exclusively for me. In fact, when he did, I could almost swear he was looking at me.

The following day, more people were in the graveyard as we passed. Men and women, well dressed, but some suits and dresses they wore seemed out of date. At first, I considered it might be an Amish or Hasidic group performing some sort of burial ritual, but over the next few days, the numbers increased. While some appeared as solid as anyone you might meet on the street, others were tougher to make out clearly. They appeared to have faded to uniform gray, clothes and all, and I swear, some seemed transparent. By the end of that week, I could perceive several hundred of them lined up beside the tombstones, about one for every five or six burial sites.

We waved at each other as we had earlier. I nearly choked when I witnessed one further back have his arm fall off as he was raising it to wave. As he passed from my sight, it seemed to me he was calmly bending over to pick it up and reattach it. That was enough for me. I went back to scanning the free newspaper for the entire journey. I was determined never to look out that train window again. It was just too damn eerie.

4

Chap. 4. Do Ya Ken Done In

The station I got off at in the morning was a short distance from my office, and unless the weather was terrible, I walked it. It was a short and uninteresting walk until they began demolishing one of the older buildings along the way. The demolition company had put up wooden barriers with windows for those who wished to enjoy what was going on behind those barriers as they passed by.

It really wasn't the most exciting thing to spend a few minutes on, but it certainly outpaced the pre demolishment route for entertainment value. That was where I met Kendrick Overjohn. Kendrick worked at the same company I did, but he was in accounting. He was a nice enough guy in his own way.

As it happened, we walked the same route to work at about the same time most days and would spend a few minutes on the sidewalk outside the demolition site. While there, we would exchange a little small talk about the progress of the demolition or the vagaries of the workplace. He was always pleasant, and I quite liked him, although he was a bit too much of an eager beaver about work for me. We would then walk the rest of the way to our office building together unless he had to rush to some important meeting or other, and they all seemed seriously important. He would then rush off ahead and be long in the building when I walked through the doors.

As the demolition progressed, I noticed a gentleman in rather old style clothes joining us at the viewing window. He would smile and nod at us, but never spoke. He seemed affable enough but was very intent on the demolition. While we talked, he watched. He, similar to Kendrick, arrived like clockwork at about the same time, usually when I was making my way along the street to join them at the viewing windows.

Then came the day of the accident. When I arrived at my usual time, Kendrick was not yet there. So, it was the guy in the old style suit peering intently through the viewing window and me looking around for Kendrick. In a gap in traffic, I could see him running towards me, but on the other side of the street. Despite a steady flow of traffic, he suddenly bolted across the road. He didn't see the taxi coming quickly along the inside lane. I yelled, but if he heard me, it was too late. The taxi driver must have seen him at the last minute and hit the brakes. There was a squeal of brakes, along with a loud thump. The taxi had no chance of avoiding him. Kendrick briefly leaned over onto the hood of the taxi, then slipped to the ground. Traffic stopped and people got out of their cars. Oblivious to all this, Kendrick picked himself up, brushed off his coat, gathered up his briefcase, and made his way over to me. Before I could ask him if he was alright, he exclaimed breathlessly, "Love to stop and chat, Brendan, but there's a big budget meeting and I'm already late," and he ran off towards the office.

"Did you see that?" I commented to the guy in the old style clothes, "I thought the taxi killed him. It must be one hell of an important meeting for him to rush on after what just happened."

"Don't worry," returned the guy, "he'll slow down when he gets to the building's main doors. In fact, he may be there for a while?"

"What do you mean?" I asked. "The doors are automatic; he'll fly right through them."

"Not too likely," he replied. "I've seen it happen before. He'll get to the door, but it won't open for him. He doesn't yet know he really could fly through it. But then, who cares? He won't have any influence in that meeting. I don't know why these people even bother."

As he spoke, an ambulance pulled up beside the still stopped taxi. A crowd of people had gathered round. "There," said the guy in the old-fashioned clothes, pointing to the crowd around the ambulance and taxi, "what do you think they're all doing over there?"

"Beats me," I replied,

"They're trying to resuscitate, but it's too late."

"Resuscitate who?" I wanted to know.

"Your harried friend."

"What are you talking about? He's gone to the office. I just saw him."

"Well, I thought you might. I was pretty sure you saw me."

I was about to ask him what the hell he was talking about, when a group of fellow co-workers who had been standing around the ambulance were coming over to me. "Don't talk to me," said the guy beside me in a hushed tone. "Don't look my way. We'll talk later."

Then I was engulfed by horrified and agitated co-workers, and that's when I learned Kendrick had just been loaded into an ambulance, and the paramedics weren't sure if there was any chance, he would survive.... And wasn't it terrible? How could anything like this happen? Someone will have to tell the accounting department....

That's when I wondered who or what I had seen running by for an important budget meeting earlier. It sure looked like Kendrick and I saw him being hit by the taxi. When I got to the office building lost in my questioning wonder, there he was, just where old style wardrobe guy had said he would be. Standing outside the main doors of the building. He had a look of confused panic on his face.

Concerned, I walked up to him, "Hey, Ken, you, ok?"

"No, Brendan, I'm not," he said. "I can't get the door to open. It's as if the sensor doesn't see me. It lets everyone else in. But not me. Would you hold the door open so I can get inside? I'm really late for the budget meeting."

I held the door for him, and he raced through and off to the elevators. I watched as he boarded the elevator; the doors closing behind him, wondering if anyone else was getting off at his floor. I was pretty sure if I waited long enough, I would see him still there when the elevator doors opened again. Then I caught myself. What was I doing being so matter of fact at the sight of a ghost? He didn't look like a ghost. He looked as solid and real as anyone else. Yet I knew, without a doubt, Kendrick was on his way to the local hospital, where he would likely be declared dead. This was very disconcerting and very weird.

I told the girl at reception to call my department and tell them it traumatized me, seeing Kendrick get hit by the taxi, and I was going home and went back out through the doors I had helped Ken through moments earlier. Walking back toward the station, I encountered Mr. Old-Fashioned Clothes guy. "So," he said, "you figure it out yet? Are you ready to talk to me now?"

17

5

Chap. 5. If the Grave Fitz

Mr. Old-Fashioned Clothes guy pointed out that the Kendrick I saw at the office doors was, in fact, the late Kendrick Overjohn. Strangely, I wasn't very surprised when he informed me, he, too, was dead. "What are you?" I asked, "Some kind of ghost?"

"Beats me," he grinned. "Whatever I am, you can see me. That's enough for me."

Not only could I see him, but I could also hear him, and I was sure that if I put my hand on him, he would feel as substantial as anyone else on the street. I knew in that instant I could see, feel, touch, and hear the dead. I had only one question, and I said it out loud, "Why?"

Ignoring my outburst, he led me over to the observation window. The remnants of the demolished building were few. He pointed over to the left rear of the pit. "See," he said, "against the wall over there, beside that pile of rubble, there is a large metallic looking plate. That's where I am, where I've been for nearly a hundred years. It's not a very comfortable place to sleep and although it doesn't matter much anymore, I would like to be out of there."

A First World War veteran, he told me he returned home from several years in the trenches. He was wounded in combat a couple of times, but the worst wounding was to his mental faculty. On his return, he spent several years in physical and mental recuperation in a local veteran's hospital. When he left the hospital, he had one suit and nowhere to stay. He began looking for work, unsuccessfully, and the best place to sleep without totally messing up his clothing was in the small tank he pointed out to me.

One night, his despair at finding no work got the better of him. He went into a local bar with his last two dollars and left very drunk. He returned to his hidey hole, as he called it, at the construction site. He climbed into the tank and fell into a drunken sleep. While he slept, oblivious to everything, the construction crew paved over the tank. When he woke up, he discovered they trapped him. He pounded on the empty walls, but to no avail. Before too long, the building enclosed his hiding place, with him permanently encased within. There, he, or what remained of him, had stayed for nearly a hundred years. Now the building was in the process of being torn down and a new one set to replace it. His resting place was outside the footprint of the new building and slated to be covered with concrete and crushed rock to lay a bed for a corporate meditation garden. "It may sound peaceful," he said, "but it doesn't help me all cramped in that tiny enclosure." He paused, took a breath and, holding out his hand, added, "by the way, they called me Fitz."

Having overcome the trepidation of shaking hands with a ghost, I admitted to him it was a tragic story, but then, curse curiosity, I just had to ask, didn't I? "Why are you telling me all this?"

His answer was about as straightforward as it gets, "Get me

out of there!"

6

Chap. 6. No Scratches Please

Yeah, I just had to ask, didn't I.

"Get me out of there," said Fitz, "and it better be soon, cause they'll be covering it up shortly, cementing over it."

"Nice to meet you, Fitz. Now, tell me, how am I supposed to get you out of there?"

"You're. a smart guy," he said, "you'll figure it out," and he was gone.

I leaned my forehead against the glass of the demolition viewing window. That's when I noticed the guy in the white hard hat down in the excavation. I'd seen him a few times talking to the workers. From their expressions, I don't think they liked him very much. One morning while I had been watching, I had seen him walking into the site. Most drove into it in their trucks and cars, but he, I discovered, left his car parked on the street. It wasn't just any car. It was the sort of machine someone like me would need to work for two lifetimes to afford the down payment. He clearly wasn't interested in driving it into the muck of the demolition site.

Between the fancy machine and the collective looks of disdain he got from the other workers, he was clearly a boss, and, I suspected, an obnoxious one. He was, no doubt, a successful engineer, perhaps even the boss. An idea germinated. I waited until he and the workers were leaving. Most drove off, ignoring him making his way up the ramp to the sidewalk. Noon seemed to worry they might splash mud on him. As he neared, I went over and stood beside his car. I could tell by his increase in speed coming up the ramp when I did this, I had his attention. "Hey," I said, as he tried to edge his way between me and the car, "You the boss man of the demolition?"

"And construction," he mumbled.

"So, what's the shiny thing at the far corner of the site?"

"What shiny thing?"

"Come over to the viewing window," I said, "and I'll show you."

"I don't have time for this nonsense," and he tried to push me out of the way.

Instead, I moved closer to the car. "Seriously," I said, "come over to the window and I'll show you."

He hesitated for a moment. I knew he would have loved to just jump in his car and take off, but I had blocked him from getting to the door. Although he tried to subtly edge his way between me and the vehicle, I stood my ground. I guess he was concerned enough that I would scratch his four wheel pride and joy's finish that he chose to go to the window with me. I assume his sudden acquiescence meant he really wanted to eliminate the risk of an odd ball scratching a several thousand-dollar paint job. "There," I said, pointing at Fitz's uncomfortable burial site.

"Damned if I know. It's not in the footprint for the new building. We'll just fill it in and pour concrete over it."

"Doesn't it look like some kind of container? Wonder what's in it?"

He seemed to think a moment, "In it?"

I had hit his curiosity button. Before I lost the moment, I added, "Remember the TV guy who did an entire show around opening a hidden cave the gangster guy built back in the twenties?"

"Al Capone," he said, "and Geraldo Rivera."

"Who?" I asked.

"Geraldo Rivera was the reporter; Al Capone was the gangster. They found nothing in the cave."

"But what if they did? Who knows what could be in that thing?"

I was counting on curiosity and greed.

The next day was Kendrick's funeral, during which he drove me nearly round the bend with all his questions about what had happened to him, and why wouldn't anyone else talk to him, and whose funeral was it, anyway. I had to tell him, "Kendrick, you're dead."

"That's hilarious, dead, me!" he said and laughed.

I left before he checked the coffin and figured it out. On my way back to the office, I stopped by the demolition site. I could see curiosity and greed had won out. The tank holding Fitz's body had been opened and a black coroner's hearse was waiting nearby. There was no sign of ghost Fitz.

I felt pretty good. A lost soul, well, actually, a lost body was found and would soon be sorted away, or whatever they do with long dead bodies they find in the walls of mercantile buildings. Not that I really wanted to know, but I would soon find out. It would be early the next morning. I came to the demolition site and stepped over to take a peek through the window.

Nothing much was happening. They had shut the job down as the police and the coroner's office checked out Fitz's now opened steel coffin. "Thanks boss."

The voice came from behind, but I recognized it and spun to face a grinning Fitz. "I owe you, boss, you did it. It was wonderful, I have to tell you, to see my bones laid out so neatly in the morgue. I could almost feel myself relaxing."

Not knowing what to say, I exclaimed, "what are you doing here?"

"Did you know," he said, "before they throw you in Potter's Field, they really seem to want to identify who you are."

"So, they've spread my bones around to two universities and the regional forensics lab. It looks like I'll be hanging around for a while yet."

That's when I noticed the guy in jeans behind him and someone beside him wearing a cheap old-fashioned suit and a gray fedora. Then I got one horrified look at a ruined face. "What the hell?" I blurted in shock.

Fitz turned casually towards it, saying, "you don't have to look like that. Just remember what you looked like back when you were alive."

Just like that, the ravaged face turned into the attractive face of a woman in her late teens or early twenties. Turning back towards me, his arm out to point at the three behind him, "I brought you some new clients."

7

Chap. 7. Put It to Rest

The first clients Fitz brought me were an interesting bunch with very different deaths and burial sites. There was a third rate petty thief, Tony Morelli, who called himself Steel. He fancied himself a big time mobster and thought the name was perfect for someone of his imagined status. I guess he hadn't heard of Joe Stalin.

Back in the '50s, he tried to set up his own little gangland. He got a bullet in the back of the head by real gangsters for his effort. He should have known better. Gangsters don't steal from other gangsters. Mobsters are primarily business managers, and their jobs from top to bottom were to take care of business.

They took care of business with the body of Steel. They put it in the trunk of his car, a Packard. They brought it to an auto wrecker and put it into the "pancake" compactor. The crusher was started, and they left. Workers at the wreckers found the car in the compactor. Although partly crushed, it wasn't completely flattened. They also discovered that the vehicle hadn't been stripped of its useful components.

They took it from the crusher and towed it to the rear of the lot, where they intended to work on it later. Later became never, and the remains of Steel Morelli stayed in the trunk of his beloved 1954 Packard Patrician 400 in a field of rusted auto parts. I only had to find the wreckers, find the car and make sure Steel's remains were discovered, then moved to a more comfortable resting place. "Piece of cake... not!"

Another was a skinny teenager named Nick. He attempted to sneak into a warehouse to do a little midnight shopping by crawling in through a large drain or exhaust pipe. He ended up stuck inside the pipe. He couldn't back up and he couldn't go forward. There was no question he regretted his intent and was both seeking reconciliation and hoping to have what remained of his earthly form exhumed from an unpleasant resting place.

Then there was Lisa Durban, attractive, scantily clad for a hot summer day. She had been picnicking with some friends at a large conservation park not too far from the city limits. During the early moments of a pickup slow pitch game, she had twisted her ankle trying to stretch a single into a double.

Although the damage to her ankle wasn't serious, there was some inflammation. It did, as she told me, "Really, really hurt."

She went to get some ice for her ankle from a cooler back at the picnic table. As she passed close to one of the many parking lots, someone grabbed her from behind and shoved a cloth full of ether against her mouth and nose. The last thing she remembered was being helped towards a car. "It was a nice car, two-tone blue and white with lots of chrome trim."

The next thing she knew, she found herself in a shallow pit under a large sheet of plywood, covered with dirt and debris that let it blend into the surroundings. When she sat up, she discovered that her upper body had passed through the plywood and its earth and tree branch covering. She climbed out of the pit, intending to run, but found as she moved away, she discovered it was a losing struggle. It was as if someone held her back, although her ankle didn't seem to hurt anymore.

As the effort became more difficult, she returned to the pit she had climbed out of. At first, she couldn't see it. There was no sign she might have climbed out. She noticed the ground close to her feet was slightly disturbed, so she reached down and found herself holding the edge of a piece of plywood. As she said, she wasn't actually holding it. She just knew it was there. As she bent over for a closer look, she was only slightly surprised when she was able to pass through the earth and plywood into a shallow grave where she saw the body of a young woman. Oddly, to her mind, was the fact body was wearing an exact copy of the outfit she was wearing. The blood stains and the vacant eyes on the body quickly informed her whoever it was lying there was dead.

She recognized an instant affinity to the body, and it shook her in that moment to realize the body was hers. It was her, and she was dead. While whatever she was now, she guessed a ghost; she felt solid enough. At least there wasn't any pain. She sat down beside the grave, waiting for something to happen. Nothing did.

She was neither hungry nor thirsty, nor did she have much awareness of the passing of time. She didn't know if she was present at the grave site all the time or went off to somewhere else. Whatever was happening, she always found herself back beside her undiscovered grave.

Over time, she noticed several others, all young women like herself. Standing or seated, guardians of similar graves. These young women, four besides her, learned they could communicate with each other. Not necessarily in words.

Their stories were like Lisa's. None of them could remember enough to know what exactly had happened to them. They assumed someone murdered them. Based on the plywood and now overgrown dirt covering it, they determined it was the same person or persons. None of the spirits of the murdered women had any idea about who the perpetrator or perpetrators were. Neither did they have any idea when their horrible turn had come.

When the spirits of the five young women appeared to be fixed at that number, they determined their murderer or murderers had, for some unknown reason, either stopped the killing spree or found a new burial site. So, the years passed and while none of them were aware of the passage of time, they could see their bodies corrupting, becoming skeletal remains.

As their bodies deteriorated, the connection that bound their ghostly selves to them seemed to similarly fade. These spirits could range farther afield. With this came the desire for a more civilized burial. I would learn later stronger emotions, especially anger and the desire for vengeance, kept the spirit earth bound but loosened the bonds to the body much quicker. Most times, if the spirit desire for revenge or some business perceived as important and needing to be taken care of, the liberation of the spirit was almost instant. That explained Kendrick, who seemed to always have important business needing taking care of.

Lisa was spokesperson for the other four, and similar to Steel and Nick and Fitz before them, all they really wanted was a decent burial. For them, a Potter's Field was better than the rusting remains of a car trunk, an exhaust pipe or a shallow grave in a woodlot. With Fitz's enthusiasm over my success in his case, the others had come to expect I would somehow discover their remains, wherever they now were, and somehow free them so they could be laid to a proper rest.

Not the sort of job I was hoping for.

8

Chap. 8. Steeling Away

Steel Morelli was not a bad guy for a bad guy, it's just his ambitions were skewed. He had no wish to be an actor, or an artist, a singer, or a wealthy business executive. He wanted to be a mobster. To be patron to a bunch of thugs, a kind of modern-day Fagin. Come on, didn't you all read Oliver Twist when you were in high school or have at least seen the old musical Oliver on the late, late show? Well, times have changed. Perhaps you didn't.

To this end, he ran a numbers scam, only it wasn't a scam. In fact, the folks in his neighborhood loved it. Not only did he pay off fairly, he would personally deliver the winnings. Business was good and, had Morelli stayed in his neighborhood, he might be mayor today. However, he didn't. Perhaps he had gotten greedy, but it is more likely he got too much encouragement from many happy customers. Some on the edge of the neighborhood, or close by, heard of Honest Steel Morelli, an interesting name for a gangster wannabe, and decided they would rather do business with him than with their regulars.

The regulars skimmed the winnings, overcharged, and could

be pretty nasty when collecting back debts. They also worked for a gang boss who didn't consider the positive social and fiscal benefits of competition. Poor Steel had barely driven his brand new Packard off the lot when the gang boss reclaimed his monopoly and began expansion into Steel's territory.

Steel really didn't deserve to die the way he did, and certainly didn't deserve to be left in the trunk of a half flattened, rusting hulk of a 1954 Packard until he and it turned to dust. I had to find the time to help him.

Think finding a body in the trunk of a 1954 Packard in some wrecking yard would be easy? Let me dissuade you of that idea right away. First of all, you can always find plenty of auto wreckers with yards near any metropolitan area.

My initial job was to narrow down those that were around and well established in 1954. It took a great deal of research and driving around to gather this information. When I finally finished the research, I could reduce the number of older auto wreckers down to ten from over thirty in the area. Most of these wreckers were established primarily for parts salvage. Any car crushing the needed was arranged to be done somewhere off site.

The places they sent them to were fairly modern, and the compacted vehicles were shipped off shortly afterwards to smelters. Only three wreckers in the vicinity ever did their own auto crushing. None of them currently did their own crushing on location, but I was able to find two that kept some remnants of compacted or partly compacted automobiles.

When I spoke to them on the phone, there was no one at either place who even knew what a Packard was, let alone know if they had one. It meant I would need to visit the wreckers looking for s crushed 54 Packard, and when was I going to find time for that?

9

Chap. 9. Steel Back

I had called around and found two places where the remains of Steel and his Packard might be. To check these places out, I needed to take some time off work, a day, perhaps two. I could see how this newly imposed career could be a problem in that regard. Between the planning and the execution, freeing the discontented dead from their unpleasant graves, was a time-consuming business.

At the moment, however, I was less worried about taking time off and more concerned with helping out someone Fitz called a client. That the client had been dead for nearly seventy years was irrelevant. They had confined his physical remains in the trunk of the crushed chassis of his own 1954 Packard. Apparently, the confinement was uncomfortable for him. How this could be the case with someone dead for that long, don't ask me. Ask him.

Only you can't ask him because you can't see him. Lucky you, I can, and since I can see him and talk to him, I believe I have to help him. That's why I took a couple of sick days off to visit two auto wreckers, in one of which the remains of Steel Morelli and his car were waiting for me to find them. So, what excuse could I make up to explain why I wanted to spend some time searching through the wreckage of old cars?

What was my reason for visiting these auto wreckers? I decided to tell them I was a collector of automobile memorabilia, especially hood ornaments. I would tell them I had an extensive collection already but was missing an ornament from the hood of a 1954 Packard Patrician. Being more or less the last of the line of that specific vehicle, the hood ornament was an essential piece for my collection. I know it was a pretty lame excuse, but I guess there were other similar collectors, because the managers immediately accepted my story at both locations.

In the first wreckers, they piled the older cars three high in one area of the lot. With some careful climbing and some small power tools, I could get several hood ornaments. I have to admit; they were pretty neat, and they were going to cost me if I was to keep my story straight.

There was no sign of Steel, skeleton or ghost, and no sign of a Packard. I paid for the hood ornaments and went on to the next auto wreckers. I was certain I would find Steel and his car in their compound.

As I mentioned, the manager bought my hood ornament collector story. Maybe he was just humoring me because it could mean a few bucks in his pocket. When I mentioned I was especially interested in the ornament from a Packard Patrician circa 1954, He told me he had heard of them, Packards, but didn't know if there were any in his yard. He asked one worker who was passing by if there were any 'different' cars around.

The worker said there were several, but if I was looking for a much older car, I might find it among the rust buckets out in the back field. He said there were a couple of partly crushed cars out there, so it might be worth a look.

The boss, the employee and I went out to take that 'look' and there it was, Steel's Packard with Steel's ghost sitting on the roof, lovingly caressing it. "It was a grand car in its day," he said to me as I approached.

The incomplete crushing of the car had sprung the trunk slightly open, and over time, Steel's now skeletal hand had pushed out through the gap. He pointed it out to me, but the others hadn't seen it. They were checking out the hood ornament that was mercifully intact, its chrome dimmed with years of dust. The employee removed the ornament, handing it to the manager, who handed it to me. They were ready to head back toward the office. I had no choice, pretending an interest in the ruined lines of the vehicle, I walked its length to the trunk and in what I hoped was my best impression of a shocked voice, called out, "My god, what the hell, that looks like a skeletal hand!"

The manager joined me at the rear of the car. "Sure, as hell does," he said, and sent the worker off to get a crowbar.

Not much later, they had pried the trunk open and, for the first time in nearly seventy years, Steel's long decomposed body was free from its uncomfortable resting place. "The back seat I could have handled," said Steel, looking down at what remained of his corpse.

The police were called and shortly thereafter, the coroners' van and a police car arrived. I stood to one side as the coroner's investigators and the police examined the body. Beside me, Steel could not stop his chatter, something else that set him apart from big time mob bosses. He was so relieved and stretched out his arms, shaking them as if working out a cramp. At last, he could feel comfortable because now his corpse, or what remained of it, was at ease. Don't ask me to explain this. Can't say it made much sense to me.

When I asked him how he was able to feel his body's resting place could be uncomfortable, he really couldn't explain it. He suggested it might be some kind of body memory he carried with him from when he first realized he was dead, and his body locked in the trunk of his car. This was about the best answer I would ever get.

While I was standing there, beside the ghost of Steel Morelli, one cop turned away from the body in the trunk and came over to me. The officer was a woman around my age. She was striking, attractive actually, in an officious sort of way. "Excuse me, sir," she asked, "are you on your cell phone?"

"No," I replied, adding out of curiosity, "why do you ask?"

"I don't know," she said, a confused look on her face, "It sounded to me like you were talking to someone named Steel asking about how the dead could feel body discomfort."

Yeah, and I was going to tell her I was conversing with the spirit belonging to the body in the car's trunk over there. I didn't know what to tell her, so I gave her about the dumbest answer anyone could. I said, "Oh, I was just thinking out loud."

She gave me a half smile and turned away. That's when I recognized her as one of the cops involved in the earlier investigation of Fitz's remains.

As the coroner's van carrying Steel's physical remains pulled out of the yard, he thanked me for everything, gave the ruined and rusty Packard one last caress, and jumped into the van to join his dusty remnants.

10

Chap. 10. The Skinny on Nick

If tracking down Steel's skeletal cadaver was a chore, finding Nick's was even more challenging. While he hadn't been trapped in the pipe at some closed down factory as long as they had trapped Steel in his car, it was long enough. So far, none of my clients could provide anything remotely resembling specific directions to where I could find their bodies. Yes, they would be at the place when I arrived, but were not much help to get me there.

First, I had to track down abandoned factories or warehouses, either near or in the city. The one thing Nick could tell me that helped was that the place, whatever it was, remained deserted. He could describe it as large and made of concrete blocks. Since his perception of size was relative, the location where he could be found might be huge, but it might also be a more modestly sized building. I couldn't use size to narrow it down, and frankly, city maps didn't point out derelict buildings.

Since I couldn't miss any more work, at least for a few weeks, I could work with Nick for a few brief moments in the evening. During that time, I did my best to keep some normality in my life. In the brief time I could work with him, he wasn't much help. He could only provide vague recollections of the building and its surroundings. Between work, middle level competitive hockey game and practice each week, not to mention pickup basketball games in the school gym on Saturdays, Nick gave me some useful information.

He told me the main floor doors were all locked and bolted inside and out, but that didn't matter. Most of the equipment on that floor had either been removed or stolen long before he broke in. He was skinny and had gone through a wide drainpipe of some sort that gave him access to the basement. That's where all the good salvage was, anyway. Over time, he took copper wire and fittings, some small machines, or parts of machinery and clean looking metal that he would bring to a local buyer.

He spent a lot of time talking about that, but I just listened for anything useful. I was neither interested nor condoning of his storied, "five finger discounts." I was more interested in listening for anything that might give me a clue how I could find this place and get someone to locate his remains. Since he only went there at night, even now, he could tell very little about the actual building. After many shared moments, he remembered part of a logo on the wall as he made his way to his secret entrance.

It was a circle with square teeth facing out and a lightning flash topped by a wrench head. Searching for the image, I learned that the toothed circle represented a gear, the lightening flash related the machines to electricity and the image of the wrench head meant the company fabricated something that used both gears and electricity. The age of the building would explain the copper that Nick could find.

Nick told me the pipe he crawled through to get in was quite large and he had gone in and out through a hundred times. He was a very skinny dude but had stopped for several months before going back again. Since he was still young, both he and I figured he must have had a growth spurt between his earlier visits and this one. The pipe curved just inside the wall and that's where he got stuck. He could neither go forward nor back up. It must have been a horrible experience, but Nick couldn't remember much of it.

All he knew was eventually he died and there he still was, after these many years. When the merely curious ghost of Nick dropped in on his decaying self, it did not upset him. He was jammed in the pipe's elbow so tight even the rats and mice couldn't get at much of him. One skeletal hand had taken the brunt of their visits and was, so he told me, nearly detached from the arm.

This gave me an idea, but first I would have to locate this building. I became a regular at a library not too far from my office. There, I researched newspapers and city files looking for the logo Nick had described. After an extensive search, I found it. It was the logo for a local company called Tyler Technical. They made small engines.

Unfortunately, their design department didn't give their product much appeal and, in the end, the market passed them by, and they closed. Over the years since then, the land and building had passed through several owners' hands, but until now, the demolition crews had stayed clear. This, I learned, might change soon. However, now that I could pinpoint where the building was, it was time to carry out my plan, or so I hoped.

I had a plan, but like any complex scheme, there were no guarantees, just a lot of hope. That went double, no triple for me. I was pretty new to this stuff. Since I was now living in the world of the walking and talking dead, it seemed there was no such thing as a simple solution. It was a complicated plan, but I decided I would give it a shot.

First, I had to get into the factory grounds. Luck was with me there. Someone had cut a lovely entrance way in the steel link fence conveniently out of sight. Next, I had to find the particular pipe hosting Nick. That was no problem. Nick was sitting on it when I arrived. Whatever they had connected the pipe to, it was nowhere to be seen. It was an open-ended pipe, large enough, but not exceptionally so. Nick had to have not only been beyond slender, but double jointed as a carnival contortionist to have ever gotten into that pipe.

With effort, I was able to twist the pipe, so it faced upward. It creaked and made a complaining rasp as I did it, but it stayed in place. Back in the trunk of my car, secreted outside the fence, I had five jerry cans filled with water. Over the next hour, I wrestled those weighty containers from the car through the gap in the fence and set them down, one at a time, beside the upturned pipe. One after the other, I emptied them into the pipe.

I knew we were in line for some heavy showers later. Between the rain and the contents of the jerry cans, I hoped the flow of water would dislodge Nick's remains. It rained heavily for the next two days. Nick kept a regular check and three days later, he showed up to tell me that the hand and part of the arm had fallen through and were on the floor beneath the interior end of the pipe.

It was time to execute the second part of the plan. Having researched the ancient factory extensively, I knew of the current owner. It was a small, but from the reviews, an ambitious company with plans to demolish the old factory and put in a state-of-the-art office building. Since they were new on the scene, they would want to avoid adverse publicity. I called them as someone who lived near the factory and complained gangs of drug addicts, or some gang members were using their factory to party. I added they might even prepare meth there.

That very day, the company's security department arrived to check the place out. There was little evidence it was a gathering place for addicts or gangs. The machine parts they found in the basemen interested them enough to have them spend some time down there. They must have been thorough, which was a benefit for us. Well, at least for Nick. They found the hand still attached to an arm. They called the police while they cut open the pipe to liberate Nick's dusty bones.

After several days examining what there was left of Nick, the coroner declared it was death by misadventure and not long after; they lay him to rest in the city's potter's field.

11

Chap. 11. Lost Ground

Finding auto wreckers around the cities and even determining their age, or searching down deserted factories, were difficult, but not impossible. The information was all there in a variety of documents that, with some effort, could be tracked down. Finding an isolated wood lot that could be anywhere, now that is something else altogether. Nope, you can't research something like that in a library.

I would have to start at the beginning, and that meant interviewing five murdered teenage girls. Lisa was the chattiest of the girls, making her the ideal spokesperson for the others. She was smart enough, but not very observant. Can't fault her there. Until I threw away my glasses, I couldn't have told you one landmark I passed on the train ride to and from work. If they gave marks for "I Spy" in kindergarten, I would have failed.

Some of the other girls were more helpful. One girl was kidnapped in a conservation area, possibly the same one Lisa was abducted from. Two other girls had been taken from a shopping mall.

The killer had carried off the fifth girl from a church parking lot where she was waiting to be picked up by her mom. She had been at a play rehearsal in the basement and came out to the parking lot with some others, but her mom was late to arrive. The others had gone, leaving her alone for a short time. She noticed a fancy-looking car parked at the back of the lot but didn't give it much thought. Like Lisa and the other girls, someone grabbed her from behind and a cloth with some smelly stuff on it, likely ether, pressed over her face. She was dragged towards the car on the verge of passing out. Being drugged, all she could recall was whoever was holding on to her was wearing glasses. She could see the glasses, but not the face, reflected in the car window. If it was a man or woman, she wasn't sure. Whoever it was, the person opened the car door and shoved her in and that's all she remembered.

When the girls abducted from the mall described it, the girl from the church was sure it was the mall close to where she lived. That was information I could check out in the library. I spent more time the next few days pouring through microfiche of old editions of newspapers than I had ever spent in the library while a student at university. I learned the girls disappeared at different times over a period of about three years, twenty or so years back. To boot, there was a popular conservation park in the vicinity where two girls had gone missing. I had a starting point.

There were vast acres of woodland beyond the conservation park. The makeshift graves could be anywhere in there, or worse, they could be anywhere within several thousand klicks. I had to begin somewhere, so I made my way to the main entrance to the park and began a tour of the back roads in the area. To me, the drive was aimless. I went from one back street to another

43

to a highway and back off the road on to another side street. I got pretty tired, so eventually, I turned around and headed for home.

There is a character in a series of books I had read by Dean Koontz. The hero of the book's name is Odd Thomas. Like me, he could see ghosts. Unlike me, he couldn't have conversations with them, but I digress. Odd Thomas had a gift. If he needed to find someone, he would just set off at random and sooner or later, usually sooner, he would meet up with the very person he was looking for. Something like that, anyway. You'll have to read the books to see what I mean. I tell this because the next day I went to the mall where the two girls were taken from. Starting from there, I made my way to the less populated back roads nearby to check them out. I had no plan, just drove. I was doing this more in frustration than with any sense of confidence I would find anything.

How it happened, I really don't know, but several hours of traveling the side roads, I ended up back at the place where I had turned to go home the previous night. Since it was fairly early on a Sunday afternoon, I headed down the road, crossed a major highway, and continued on. Not too far along, I discovered something else about my improved, or should I say, different vision, I could see a greenish glow off in the distance, as I passed an old farmhouse, I came to an overgrown field and beside it what looked like a badly neglected apple orchard. Pulling up to it, the greenish glow differentiated into five separate columns located among the trees.

I stopped the car and got out. The fence was nothing more than a set of rotted logs that had collapsed in many places, making for an easy entrance to the field. I made my way to the first column of green light. Sitting cross-legged on the ground, surrounded by the light, was Lisa. She looked up and waved. "Oh great," she grinned, "you found us." The other girls immediately appeared and were standing around me. One of them softly implored, "So now, can you please get us out of here?"

"Not so easy," I replied. "I have no reason to be here. They could charge me with trespassing, and there is a lady cop who has expressed some interest in me, and it's not the kind of interest I like."

Neither Lisa nor the others said anything. Lisa just gazed at me and pouted. "Don't worry," I said, trying more to convince myself than the girls, "I'll get you out. It's just going to take a little time. You've been here for years. You can wait a little longer."

Her pout grew more intense, and she looked down. "I guess," she muttered.

"I promise," I said, but at the moment I was uncertain about that.

October was beginning, and the weather was going to be nice. The forecast was promising more sunshine and more warm days. There had to be some way to get Lisa and the others out of their graves before it got too cold, and the snow came. I was sitting at my desk with some work spread out across it I wasn't looking at. Instead, I was wracking my brain trying to come up with a way to help five girls long buried in shallow graves under rotting sheets of plywood, soil, and piles of dead leaves. When something came to me, it was like magic.... Just kidding.

The company I worked for was a forward-looking establishment. There were several social committees, and they expected the employees to join and support them. These committees were intended to assist in corporate community building. I guess I can admit that I was rather jaded about such things, so to me it was just a well thought out plan to turn us working stiffs into a family, a happy, well-coordinated team to joyfully improve the profit margins. It was, I have to say, a good idea. Social events were big time popular with this company and admittedly, it made it a great place to work.

When the company hired me. I signed up for the social activity group, then promptly forgot about it except for the occasional meeting they called me to attend. While I was sitting at my desk looking for a brilliant solution to my dilemma and at that point any solution would be brilliant, a fellow worker came by to remind me the social activity group would meet just before quitting time. Eureka, I had it! Well, no, I didn't. However, by the time I got to the meeting, something in the back of my brain was germinating. It certainly wasn't a thought in the front of my brain until I heard someone mention, "while the weather was good, we should do an outdoor activity, but it should be something different."

I couldn't restrain myself. "Orienteering," I shouted.

Everyone turned to look at me, their eyes wide and a look of astonishment on their faces. Until then, I had contributed nothing to the meetings. Before that day, my contribution to the committee included drinking the company provided orange juice, eating the free donuts and making small talk with others like me who were only there because they kinda had to be. After all this time, I finally had something to say. I'm sure I confused everyone, but they listened. "Hey," I said, "we find a woodlot somewhere outside the city. It's been a lovely fall, and the trees look quite nice and colorful right now. We get some teams together, give them compasses and maps. They race through the checkpoints; everyone gets a little prize and then we have a picnic."

"Or, find a nearby restaurant," said one of the less outdoorsy of the committee.

"Absolutely," I agreed.

"Ok," said miss serious, the chairperson, "Who wants to take that on?"

If the committee members' eyes went wide before, they nearly fell right out when I said, "I will."

12

Chap. 12. Seekers Finders

Since the dead came into my life, I have spent more effort in libraries doing research than I ever did back at school, or at my nine-to-five work. Between the microfiche and the city documents, I have learned a lot. A good thing, too. Unknown to my fellow social activity committee members, I had to track down an owner because I had a particular place in mind for the activity I had volunteered to lead. As it turned out, the owner of the farmhouse close to the old apple orchard lived in a house not too far away.

I phoned him, and he was very obliging. He suggested I drop by, and he would give me a handwritten permit should anyone question me. Turns out he had only lived there a short time. His aunt and uncle owned the house he was in and the farm it included as well. They also owned the neighboring farm with the ancient stand of apple trees. No one had lived there for many years. He told me they had rented it out several times to different people. Currently, the house was in poor condition and was dangerous. He was considering pulling it down but hadn't gotten to it yet. As for the overgrown grounds, he had been an aviation technician living and working in a factory out west. He was not a farmer and had no interest in becoming one, so the land, like many of the farms around, would remain as it was, slowly being overgrown.

He gave me the certificate for use and asked me to guarantee not to hold him responsible should there be an accident. I called our company legal advisor, who told me what to write to confirm the landowner would not be held responsible for any accident that occurred to anyone covered by the certificate of usage. I thanked him and drove back to the woodlot that was mostly an overgrown apple orchard. Over the next few hours, I plotted out several routes through the trees and surrounding woods. All these routes would, all things being equal, take about the same time to complete. I designed each of these routes to have the participants pass directly over at least three of the burial places. Given the state of the plywood and the likely condition of the shallow grave and its occupant, at least one pair of contestants would step on one and break through. Yeah, it would bring the orienteering picnic to a quick and unfortunate end but revealing even one burial location would be all that was needed to liberate the five unfortunate girls buried there.

Meanwhile, back at the office, the committee spread ads for the Orienteering social throughout the building. The ads caught the interest of a large group of fellow employees. In the end, there were twelve pairs of competitors and another nine volunteers to help monitor the run. Four others were maintaining the reservations at a not too distant restaurant. Along with the committee members, including myself, there would be about forty people to provide witnesses to any unexpected and unpleasant discovery. The day picked for the event was perfect, and when we got to the location, many of the fallen apples were

49

lovely and crisp. And, probably wormy, so we let them be.

Happy, eager pairs took compasses and maps and were ready to start. When everyone taking part was at the starting line, miss serious who was less serious this morning, called out in her loud, but modest, official voice, "Go."

Laughing and shouting in excitement, the teams were off. Everyone could hear them as they ran, "This way."

"No, that way."

"Look at the map."

"Is that the right direction?"

As the organizer, my job was done. I now had the luxury to relax, pour myself a ready-made coffee and wait for the scream. A half hour and two coffees later, the distance sound of laughter suddenly turned into a cry of surprise, maybe pain. There were several moments of silence followed by the awaited scream. A second one followed moments later from another direction. They were not screams of delight. Moments later, the fun and games were over. No one had lost an eye or suffered a major injury, but there were some scratched and bloody ankles. A pervasive sense of horror hung over everyone. Miss serious, whose actual name was Astella Weismann, called the police.

A member of the local police showed up and took a quick look around. Then, he made a call on his cellphone, not the noisy machine in the car. He asked us to hang around because specialized investigators from the city and the coroner would arrive shortly. They would want to speak with us. I shuddered, suspecting the policewoman who had spoken with me at two other body finds would be among those specialists.

While there were a few who hadn't seen the burial sites. Most stayed well away, but some of the more curious had shifted the plywood on one and looked in. Their inspection, in every one of their cases, was brief. Most were back at the start location extremely fast. Eating was out of the question. Coffee and other more warming drinks became popular. There was a lot of chatter, but the noisiest one was Lisa and only I could see and hear her as she danced around me whooping her pleasure. "You did it. I'm found!" And she kept kissing me, and one time even swung me around. It would have looked mighty odd to anyone watching, but no one was.

The special investigation unit, or whatever the cop who came earlier called it, arrived just ahead of the coroner's black van. The investigators were in plain clothes. The one wearing the severe black pant suit was one I had seen before, at least twice. As I mentioned before, she was attractive in a serious sort of way. She had showed up with her fellow officers when Fitz's body was discovered, and she was one of those who had come when I liberated Steel. I don't know if she was there when Nick's remains came out of the pipe, but I suspect she was.

I wasn't happy to see her. She was the one who spoke to me when Steel was found, and I suspected she might recognize me. I tried my best to slip into the background; stand off to the side, but Lisa followed me and once again began shouting, "I'm free. Brendan did this for me," and planted a kiss on my cheek.

Just as Lisa yelled, the policewoman spun to look my way. I tried to shift so she wouldn't see me head on, but Lisa wasn't leaving me much room. While the other police officers and the coroner's crew were busy with those who had found the graves, she walked over to me. I was right, she remembered me, "You still thinking out loud?" she asked.

I guess Lisa was so excited about being liberated from her shabby resting place that she got a little silly and said to the policewoman as she approached, "Take a hike, lady cop,

51

Brendan's my guy."

The policewoman looked startled. To tell the truth, I was too. The lady cop, as Lisa called her, took a quick look around to see who had spoken. There was no one nearby. "Did you say that?" she asked. "Are you some kind of smart assed ventriloquist?"

She reminded me of my sixth-grade teacher. I responded to her just as I would answer to Miss Jermaine, "No ma'am, sorry," then added, because I always felt the need to explain, "I'm just a bundle of nerves from all this. Makes me a bit Tourettic."

Lisa laughed and punched me on the arm. It made me wince, turn toward her and rub my arm. The policewoman stared at me and my odd gyration. Then her manner changed. She reached into her jacket and pulled out a calling card. Handing it to me, she said, "I want you to call me at this number."

I stared at her in disbelief. Why would she want me to call? Was I a suspect or something? I was too shocked to ask. All I could say was, "I work tomorrow."

"That's fine, any time during the week is good," and with that, she turned back to join her fellow officers.

Lisa was still bubbling, but I didn't notice. My mind was down in some dark hole. Could she arrest me or have me charged for something? I visualized images straight off the TV with me in a small room, my wrists shackled to the table with chains while she interrogated me.

13

Chap. 13. Murder He Said

The police had spotted me at least twice at human remains recovery sites, or at least one police officer did. She had given me her card. She was detective Jennifer Wenstead from central office, meaning she was a specialist and she wanted to talk to me. I didn't want to talk to her, so as soon as I got home, I took her card and threw it into the garbage pail. Less than a moment later, I had second thoughts and fished it out. I brought it to my bedroom and put it in the top drawer of my dresser. I shoved it to the back, covering it up with assorted loose papers and old glasses cases.

On my way to work the next morning, I saw Fitz looking through the window at the construction of the new building that swallowed up the grave that held him for nearly a hundred years. This is where I usually saw him. Where we would briefly talk about any ideas I had in planning and exposing the remains of what he termed my "clients."

This time, when I saw him, I told him the police were getting uncomfortably interested in me. I told him I wanted to lie low for a while so, for now, would he please not find me any new clients? For me, 'for now' meant forever, for him, not so long. Nevertheless, he agreed. That was good. I could avoid those spirits seemingly all around me as long as I looked straight ahead or had my eyes down, reading. This provided me some respite from the spirits of the dead, some of whom could be, to say the least, annoying.

Several weeks passed with none of the dearly departed, including Fitz, intruding on my serenity. It was a lovely break. The time spent planning and supporting the reclamation of the earthly remains of Fitz, Steel, Nick, Lisa, and the four other girls had taken a lot out of me. This time provided me with a chance to relax, as well as to keep me clear of detective Wenstead.

I was getting used to this. I was just starting to feel I had gotten my old life back. That lasted right up to the morning several weeks later when I walked into my kitchen to find a man in a business suit seated on the edge of the table. "You have to help me," he said matter-of-factly.

"Fitz." I called and there was Fitz beside me.

"Fitz, I thought I told you, no more clients for now," I admonished, "I told you I wanted to lie low for a while."

For a moment, it seemed Fitz was going to cry, "Sorry, boss, I had nothing to do with this guy. He found you all on his own."

"I'm having some 'me' time," I told the business suit, "I'm not ready to go rescuing remains. You'll just have to wait in your hidey hole a while longer."

"Not in a hidey hole," he said.

"Then," and there I went, running off at the mouth again, "why are you here?"

"I want you to turn my murderer over to the law."

"Your murderer," I gasped, "you were murdered?"

"Yep," he responded, "I was murdered."

"And you want me to find your murderer?"

"No, I know who he is," he said, his voice rising. "I just want him away from my wife and behind bars where he belongs."

He told me he didn't mind his wife finding another companion now that he was gone, but not the one who had murdered him. Although, as he admitted, that relationship was one reason why he had been killed. That, and the fact that not so long before he was killed, he had beaten out his murderer for a big and very lucrative promotion. "Why me?" I asked.

"Because you can see me, and I can talk to you. I can show you the creep and tell you exactly where he is going to be at any given time. I can tell you a lot of details...."

"That I couldn't possibly know!" I interrupted, "If I brought it to the police, they'd either laugh me out of the place, or when they found the body where I told them it was, they would make me prime suspect and lock me away," I was not happy with either prospect.

"Then you're going to need your spidey sense to figure it out, aren't you?" Then, with a snort, that might have been a laugh and, "I'll be in touch," he vanished.

I stared at Fitz, who was looking off in the direction my murdered visitor had turned before disappearing. Going after murderers, it was all a bit much.

There was a bottle of whiskey on the top level of my bookshelf. It had sat there for several years, but suddenly it had become very important to me. I pulled it down and poured myself a glass, then indicated the bottle with my hand and nodded at Fitz, "Oh lord. Would I love to," he smiled, "but it's one drawback of my current condition. I can't eat or drink, or even sip a wee drop of whiskey."

"Well, I can," I said and took a healthy swig of the burning fluid.

The next day was Saturday, so I would not be going to work, ahh, weekends. I could spend the day in my small, superbly furnished apartment, meaning the sixty-inch television, the comfortable chair I bought when I moved in, and the tatty old sofa my parents had given me. They had obviously wanted it out of their house, but it worked for me. However, when I looked into the refrigerator for a snack, it was nearly empty and what there was either inedible or moldy. a stark sign a shopping trip was in order. Since I lived minutes away from the shops and the largest mall in town, I walked.

On my way to the grocery store near some smaller stores and flirting with the mall next door, I came to a small shop looking like it had been there for fifty or more years. The title on the window read Kwick Optometry. It may have looked like it was there for years, as it blended perfectly with its tacky surroundings. Maybe so, but I swear, I had walked that block thousands of times, and never noticed it before.

I further swear it was exactly the same shop front as the one I had visited back in the city. I couldn't stop myself. I had to look inside. And there it all was, just like before. The small counter, with some eye glass frames and a box of loose eyeglass parts. One shelf with a very limited and, to my mind, hideous looking collection of glasses. Unless I was experiencing Deja vu, it was the nondescript lady with straight, grayish blonde hair, excessive eye shadow and bright red lips, wearing a gray cardigan with the emblem of some university or college behind the counter. Is a there such a thing as identical twin shops? Because. it sure seemed to be. I had to look back out the door to make sure I was still in my hometown... weird.

14

Chap. 14. Kwick

I was certain it was the same nondescript lady with straight, grayish blonde hair, excessive eye shadow and bright red lips, wearing a gray cardigan with the emblem of some university or college who I had seen in the identical twin of this shop back in the city. She looked up from whatever she was doing, saw me, and smiled. Then, as if she was expecting me, she said, "Ah, Mr. Bannon, it's you. Dr. Dabra is ready to see you now. You can go on through."

She pointed to the door into the small room where I had met the Dr. The last time. Somehow, I knew when I stepped through that doorway, I would be in the same room where I first met Dr. Dabra in before. And there it was: a threadbare patient chair and a couple of odd pieces of equipment. It should have surprised me, but I didn't. Standing beside the aged dentist chair was white-haired and shaggy, mustached Dr. Dabra. The same Dr. Dabra from the city, "Mr. Bannon, so good to see you. I understand your vision is quite excellent. Here," he said, pointing to the chair, "Sit down and we'll take a look."

He flipped the binocular looking device towards me and waved for me to look into it. I did. There was a familiar click, and he took it away. "There," he said, "that should help you a little."

Needless to say, I was confused, not only by his comment, but by the fact I was in what could only be the same store I had been in months earlier, only in a much different location. When I asked Dr. Dabra about it, all he said was, "Well, we do get around."

Apart from a half smile from the doctor, that was all I got about that, so I asked him what he meant by saying, "that should help you a little."

"Ah, yes. Well, you may have noticed when you were looking for the bodies that you research, and your senses led you straight to them. You may have even seen a green glow. They are aura bursts and come off dead bodies, but," he added, "they only show when you, and I mean you, are looking for them. Otherwise, the local graveyard and all the cemeteries would look to you like a massive green firework displays and would keep you awake all night. Your sight is improving, and you are going to be seeing auras. You will find they will tell you a lot about the owner. Their auras will help you locate murderers and what you might think of as evil spirits."

Frankly, despite his smile and friendly demeanor, none of what he was telling me sounded good. It was bad enough rescuing uncomfortable corpses. I wanted nothing to do with murderers, and especially evil spirits. When I informed him of my feelings, he laughed. "Sorry, young man, but these are the consequences of the line of business you have chosen to follow."

I don't remember making any such choice. In fact, given a legion of choices, it was not one I would have considered for even a moment. I asked him what he was talking about, and why me. His answer was terse, "When you revealed your sight, you made the choice."

I didn't remember that option being presented at the time, and I told him so. He smiled as he said, "If it wasn't your choice, you wouldn't have gained the sight. So perhaps I should say, it chose you."

"Lucky me," I couldn't hide the sarcasm n my tone, "Just what I needed, to be chosen to see and serve dead people."

"Oh, no," said Dr. Dabra, "It's not like that. Those people who see and serve dead people are undertakers, funeral directors, and morticians. Your role is nothing like that. They can't talk to them, you can and anyway, you're not seeing dead people, you are seeing living spirits."

"Yeah, well, those living spirits are going to get me jailed. A police officer has already approached me."

"Yes, of course, Detective Wenstead. We gave her a vision upgrade not so long ago. Perhaps a few months before you. She never quite developed the sight as well as you have, but she can sense spirits nearby, hear them sometimes, and she has a good range of aura recognition. It might do you well to meet up with her. You know, keep you out of trouble, avoid uncomfortable stays in local lockups, etcetera. Something you might want to consider now that you've moved into the world of the murdered and the murderers."

Well, that explained her interest in me; it wasn't just my being around the discovery site of more than one set of remains; it was my conversations with the spirits that caught her attention. Although the thought of getting tight with a severe and austere police officer didn't really appeal to me, I presume it would be better than an uncomfortable stay in the local lockup, something I knew I wouldn't much care for. Not long after the encounter with Doc Dabra, I was searching through my dresser for Detective Wenstead's card. As to the Kwick Optometry shop, I passed its location as many times afterwards as I had before, and I never saw it there again. It had vanished completely, the dust webs, the ancient brochures, the dead flies in its display window, and all.

Deciding to phone, I picked the old land line from what I always thought would be its final resting place in the bookshelf beside the TV and sat it on the table. Having taken it to the coffee table, I knew I would eventually have to make the call. At the moment, however, I was doing my best to avoid it. I dawdled about for what seemed like hours, well, at least ten minutes. The phone, despite my hoping, had no intention of doing anything useful but simply sit there, so I picked it up and held it to my ear. There was a pleasant, but uninteresting dial tone, and again, nothing happened. Was I putting off making the call? Of course, I was. I would have to make it sooner. At the moment, however, I might as well have been the shy fourteen-year-old me trying to get up the nerve to call Marianne Todd to ask her to be my date for the frosh dance. Flash, I never did, although she did go to prom with me two-and-a-half years later. Right now, I have a murdered spirit chasing me around looking for relief. I couldn't wait two-and-a-half years to make the call.

I had dialed all but the last number, hung up and dialed it again several times before keying in the final number. Then the phone was ringing. Oh, I was really hoping for an answering machine, but before I could hang up, a crisp officious voice said, "Wenstead."

The fourteen-year-old me swallowed and squeaked out, "Officer Wenstead, it's Brendan Bannon. You asked me to call you some time back. I don't know if you remember?"

"Yes, Mr. Bannon, I remember you. I would like to meet up for a chat. I'm working today, but I'm off tomorrow. Could we meet somewhere, maybe for coffee."

Crap, it was like a date. I swallowed and responded, "yes, that would be fine."

Since it would be Saturday, we decided on a popular coffee shop we both knew, close to my office building. I could take the commuter train down. Yeah, the one they call the Shopper Express. I'm a grown man, and yet I felt like a timid teenager about to go on my first date.

15

Chap. 15. Ally

Saturday morning and I was riding the Shopping Express, making my way from home to the city just as I had most days during the week for the last few years. If there were any dead people, sorry, living spirits of dead people, waving at me, I didn't see them. I was lost in thought, and to be honest, feeling a mite nervous about what was to come. It was a cloudy day and there was a light dusting of snow as I walked from the station to the coffee shop for the rendezvous with detective Wenstead.

Whatever Dr. Dabra had done to my vision, one thing I did appreciate was how quickly my eyes adjusted to the dark after coming in from the bright morning sun. I did a scan of the room and there was no one there who even remotely resembled the police officer I was looking for. I ordered a large latte and found a booth where I could watch my surroundings and check the door for new arrivals.

Saturday morning at the coffee shop, and from what I could see in the booths and at the stools, I was not only the youngest person in there besides the baristas, but my dad would also have been the second youngest. As I watched the door, it opened, and a laughing couple came through. I have to say their behavior may have been young at heart, but otherwise they fit in perfectly with the rest of the crowd. Stepping in immediately behind them was a very attractive young woman casually dressed wearing blue Jeans and a graphic sweater promoting a famous brand name. It first I thought she was another barista coming on duty, but she stopped just inside the doorway and looked around. She looked familiar, and I shortly knew why, as she approached me.

Detective Wenstead came to the booth, looked at me and asked, "Brendan Bannon?"

She was anything but the business-like cop who had given me her card. I was flabbergasted, if that is a proper word, because it expressed exactly how I felt. I was speechless and just nodded. "Good," she said with a smile. "Sorry I'm late, rough morning. Hang on while I get a coffee."

"That," said a voice in my ear, "Is one handsome looking lady cop."

"Fitz," I whispered, "be quiet, she can hear you and nowadays we say police officer. In fact," I added, "why don't you scram."

"Sorry, boss," he said wistfully, "but you have to admit...," and he disappeared.

"I beg your pardon; did you say something to me?" She was back at the booth with a large coffee in her hand.

"No," I laughed, "just thinking out loud."

"Yes," she said with a knowing grin, "you seem to do that a lot," and, damn it, she chuckled.

It was a lovely sound, and I could feel my cheeks heating up. "Yeah," I said, "I guess I do."

She sat down, removed her shoulder bag and reached in to pull out a notebook and pen, set it on the table beside her, but didn't open it. She took a long sip of coffee, put the cup down.

"There, that's better," she said.

She picked the cup up again but held it without drinking and looked at me. "So, what made you decide to call me? I was convinced you had thrown away my card."

"Almost did but like to keep my options open."

"Why did this become an option?" She tilted her head to the side as she said this and for a brief second, I could see her cop look flash, if ever so briefly.

"To tell you the truth, I never thought I would call you until a certain Dr. Dabra suggested I should."

There was an immediate look of recognition. "Dr. Dabra of Kwick Optometry?"

"That's the one," I said, "the Kwick and the gone."

She nodded her head in agreement and then I began telling her what he had told me about her. There was a brief look of panic in her eyes as they quickly flicked around the room. "So," she asked, "what's that to you?"

I explained to her that while she could sometimes hear spirits and could sense their presence, I, on the other hand, actually saw them, could touch them, hear them, and even locate their bodies if the green glow over the girls' shallow graves was not my imagination. I made it clear it wasn't just imagination. She listened with interesting, then disarmingly said, "You weren't really thinking out loud where you. I thought so," then added, "and you needed to tell me you see dead people."

"According to Dr. Dabra, they aren't dead people, they are living spirits."

"Dead people, living spirits... six of one... So why tell me?"

"Frankly," I said, "I thought you were on to me. My deceased friend in the booth over by the door to the ladies thinks I am a valuable commodity. He brings me what he calls clients. So far, people whose bodies by accident, or design were not properly buried, wanted me to liberate their remains so they can have a decent burial even if it's in a potter's field."

"So why tell me?" She asked again.

"If I keep showing up at these sites where human remains are found, someone is going to get suspicious... someone like you, who I know, already suspects I had some unexplained part in the discovery."

"No one can consider you a suspect. These deaths were well before your time."

"Yeah, but will they always be? If it's more recent and its murder, I could find myself in a lineup. I don't want that. And now, even worse, I have a spirit calling himself Jerry Rickert, hanging around me who claims he was murdered. He says he wants me to catch his killer. Look, I don't know what your role is and why you showed up at all those sites. I bet you were at the factory where the remains were in the pipe."

Her look was incredulous. "You knew about that, too?"

I nodded my head. Well, she said, since it's confession time, I guess I should make mine. My dad was a cop and my granddad, too. They didn't make any moves up the chain of command. I wanted to follow in their footsteps, but uniform wasn't for me. I wanted to do something more, so I applied for detective. They were in no rush to promote a woman or, as one of the deputy chiefs said, "girl," like me. But I blew through all the bells and whistles. Exam results, top of the class.

Still, it worried me my vision was not quite twenty twenty. I could get away with contact lenses, but I also needed glasses. I no more than thought about it when on the way home from work I discovered Kwick Optometry. What possessed me to go in there... I swear it was a hole in the wall... I'll never know, but before I knew it, Dr. Dabra had me look in the binoculars or whatever the hell it was. Well, it worked. I don't need glasses anymore, but I also see auras around people, sense unseen presences and hear noises and sometimes talking that no one else ever seems to hear. Thanks to this, they made me detective in charge of investigating the odd old bodies that show up. It's not a job any of the male officers like.

When I saw you there in the woods where they unearthed the girls' bodies, I sensed presences around you and remembered having the same feeling earlier at the wreckers, and that's how you caught my attention. You have a very soothing blue aura with an amber outer layer, by the way."

We talked for a good long time. In fact, she was getting ready to leave. She put the unwritten in notebook and its accompanying pen back in her bag, then stopped. "You said something about catching a murderer."

I had to confess that I was doing my best to avoid any contact with spirits when he showed up. He promised me the story, but I didn't have it yet. "You have my card. When you know more, call me."

Well, it wasn't like I had a girlfriend, although she was a lovely Rita, but now I had a real female contact, who was with the police and, hopefully, would save me from potential prosecution by association down the road.

16

Chap. 16. But You're Dead

I had a professor of history in university who said, "You really get to know someone better after they're dead, because that's when their secrets all come out."

I realize he was talking to a bunch of freshmen taking a survey of history course, but for me, there is more than a small ring of truth to it. I got to know Fitz well because he was never very far away, or at least never seemed very far. All I needed to do was merely whisper his name, and he was there. As often as not, he would show up without me saying anything. As disconcerting as this could be, it was far less perturbing than when Lisa Durban showed up.

Fitz knew enough not to appear and talk to me when I was around people. Lisa's appearances were random and often badly timed. She would show up at my pickup hockey games and cheer for me. On the volleyball court, she was constantly directing me. I certainly didn't care for the fact she would appear beside me in the change room or outside the shower. I know no one else could see her, but it didn't prevent her from being an annoying distraction for me, especially when she couldn't stop talking.

Whenever those visits occurred, I had to cautiously avoid looking at her or talking to her. Whenever she appeared and walked arm in arm with me, particularly when the weather was cold and snowy. I couldn't help but feeling strange, me bundled up in my winter clothes, her in her short shorts and tank top.

When I asked her why she was still hanging around, she would tell me it was because I was her hero. The reality was, until properly laid to rest, the spirits had a bond with their bodies. Fitz could hang around because forensics had spread some of his remains between various departments and a couple of local universities, hoping to identify him. I could have told them, but who'd believe me.

I discovered from Lisa her killer had claimed a souvenir, the tip of her right baby finger from the joint to the end, and because it hadn't been found yet, she stayed around. When I asked if it was the same for the other girls, she said whoever the murderer was, he or she took a similar souvenir from them. Where were they? I wondered. "Oh," she told me, "They're gone. The missing piece was so small, they didn't need to stay. "

I asked her about people who had amputations. Did they have to hang around? "Oh no," she said, "they can go. Most don't want to stay. No one can hear or see them. It's not much fun."

Why she was still around? I wanted to know. She giggled and disappeared. But I did learn a bit about her. She was raised in a strict, religious family and this outing had been her very first, although she had recently turned twenty. She had quite an argument to get her parents to let her go. If it wasn't that some of the girls from her Church were going, she wouldn't have been allowed. As it was, she left wearing modest clothes, track pants and medium sleeved sweatshirt. Underneath it she was wearing the short shorts and the tank top I see her in. One of the girls was driving them and, once in the car, Lisa divested herself of her modest outer attire.

She was by nature and by nurture, a shy girl, pretty, but very reserved. She could barely speak to a boy, let alone go out with one. This picnic with her friends and others from the college she was attending was, for her, a coming out party. Sadly, her coming out was cut brutally short. She couldn't remember anything about what happened to her, and it was probably a good thing. The media said the young women were raped and severely beaten before they died.

On some level, I could relate. I was shy as well, and although I had girlfriends, I hadn't gotten close to anyone. But now, my heightened perception made me realize I was more popular with the girls than I thought. The pink tendrils on their auras were a dead giveaway. When I saw that, I knew they were interested, knowing that and after my experience with exposing the unmarked and uncelebrated burial sites, I had found more courage and could talk to them.

One night during our after game visit to one of the locals, I met up with a young lady I had dated in high school and visited from time to time when we were home from university. We got to talking over old times and those tiny pink tendrils grew and reach toward me. Before I knew it, we were making our way back to my apartment.

I opened a fresh bottle of wine for her and a beer for me, and we talked and laughed. When she moved from the easy chair to sit beside me on the sofa, I could feel the anticipation. She snuggled up beside me and moments later, we were in a passionate embrace. That's when I heard, "Brendan, what are you doing? I thought you loved me."

I broke from the embrace, and there was Lisa, standing beside the armchair. She was crying. "I love you so much, Brendan," she sniffled. "You are the only person I could ever talk to. You love me, don't you? You never invited me to your apartment like this."

I was dumbfounded. I had pulled away from my guest and was staring at, for her, an unseen Lisa frowning and stamping her foot. "What's wrong?" she asked with a look of concern.

"Nothing," I lied, and turned back towards her, and that's when Lisa grabbed my arm and pulled me half off the couch.

"Why don't you do this with me?" She demanded.

In that moment, I lost my cool and my wariness around ghosts, "You're dead," I said in an agitated voice, "And you were already twenty before I started kindergarten."

"What are you saying?" said my shocked guest, "Who are you talking to. I'm not dead."

"No, no," I reached out to touch her, and she shrank away, "not you."

Then, as stupid as the excuse I had given detective Wenstead, I said, "No, no, you just made me think of something I'd forgotten."

"Forgotten what?" She cried, jumping to her feet. The pink tendrils had turned to gray. "Are you sure you're alright? Listen, it's been nice talking with you, but it's late. I have to go. I'll call a taxi and wait for it in the lobby. Night, Brendan, it's been real," and she was out the door.

Lisa had an expression of satisfaction as she followed her out with her eyes. "Come on," she said, throwing her arms around me, "Kiss me like you were kissing her, and then, maybe later," she winked.

"Maybe later what?" I exclaimed, "What are you thinking? I know you're not wearing much, but you can't take it off. I was getting along so well with Carol. Now my social life is over. Let me say it again, Lisa, we can't have a relationship like that because you're dead. Not to mention you'd be way older if you were still alive."

Tears streamed down her face, but, "Humph," was all she said and vanished. As did my newfound social life.

17

Chap. 17. Get Him

Lisa seemed to be completely gone and the best I could get from Carol whenever I encountered her was a distant, but polite nod. She must have spoken to some others as the pink tendrils of their auras like hers had blended together with a distinctly green tinge and it wasn't envy.

Except for the post game outings, I talked more with Fitz than anyone else. Imagine how depressing it can be. Your only regular companion is someone who has been dead for about a hundred years. When no one else but you could see or hear him, it's about as pathetic as you would think. Like an adult with an imaginary friend. That was my life. I was otherwise on hiatus from the spirits of the dead. The only spirit beside Fritz, and until recently, Lisa, imposing himself on me during that time, was one who had been murdered and wanted me to catch his killer. No thanks, who would want to go looking for a murderer on their own. Not me!

But damn! He was persistent. He would appear as many as three or four times a day, becoming more and more insistent that I help him. He showed up in the morning while I was riding the train to the city. He was at my desk when I arrived. Sometimes he would even meet me at the coffee cart in the reception area. I couldn't have a peaceful lunch or converse with my fellow workers without him interrupting. It was driving me nuts. I wanted to scream. I wanted to beg him to get lost, to ask him why he wouldn't leave me alone. And one evening after he had come to me at least six times, I did.

"Because," he said, gritting his teeth, "my wife will marry that evil prick in a few weeks and the thought of it nauseates me. He killed me, for crap's sake!"

"What can I do?" I cried in frustration, "How can I catch a murderer I should know nothing about? If I told the police the stuff you told me, I would become their prime suspect. How else could I know all that?"

"Don't you have your cop buddy now? Couldn't she help you out?"

How the hell did he know that? "Fitz," I snarled.

He was immediately there, eyes downcast, a sheepish look on his face. "Fitz, I thought we were working together here."

"Sorry, boss, he was just so persistent. Wanted to know everything about you. He kept asking questions. I couldn't stand it. He asked me if you knew any policemen and I told him about the detective. I'm sorry. He beat me down. He was worse than my sergeant at Argonne in '18, 1918, that is."

"Yeah," I said, "I kinda figured that," and I had to admit the guy could be incredibly annoying. It looked like I was back into the spirit of things, so I went to hunt down Detective Wenstead's calling card.

We met two days later at the same coffee shop, and I outlined the story the murdered guy had told me. She took lots of notes and told me she would look into it. She called me about three days later. What she told me was something I really didn't want to hear. She must have been in the office because she talked cop. "Yes, there is a file on the person you are inquiring about, sir. His case is in the hands of missing persons, not homicide. It's being handled by another division. I'll give you the number if you want to call them."

She knew I wouldn't. "Thanks," I said, "that is not good news. I'll talk to you later."

"Very good, sir," she said, "thanks for calling. We appreciate your concern," she added a goodbye and hung up.

I didn't know if I would hear anything more from her later, but it didn't matter. I knew that the different divisions didn't like to stick their noses into another division's business. It looked as if Detective Wenstead would not be much help, at least officially. It kinda meant that if I was going to pursue it, and heaven knows, the murdered guy was damned insistent, I would do most of it on my own... with some spirited help. Usually I like my little puns, but that one fell flatter than the tires on Steel Morelli's '54 Packard.

I really didn't want to do or say anything that might implicate me. Apart from what this guy's spirit had told me, I knew nothing about the guy when he was alive, never met him, never knew he existed. Big deal, I would certainly be exonerated, but lord knows, if I shot my mouth off with all those details no one else but the murderer could know, who could tell what I would have to go through before being cleared. Wenstead might have helped, but now...?

Meanwhile, Jerry Rickert, the murdered guy, was getting more agitated. Now he was with me nearly every minute of the waking day and sometimes in the middle of the night, calling to me, "What's the holdup? What are you waiting for? The wedding is getting closer. Why haven't you got the guy yet?"

18

Chap. 18. The Story

All I knew from Rickert was that a fellow co-worker named Fred Meecham murdered him. According to Rickert, Meecham was a mean and jealous, and I quote here, "fucking greedy son of a bitch."

If what Rickert told me was true, he must have been. Meecham was a cool and calculating killer, according to Rickert. The murder had been planned out to the last detail. Meecham would travel for work from time to time. This time, he took the train to a small city not too far away. Rickert and his wife Margie were living a pleasant and peaceful life in their suburban home. Unknown to them, Meecham had rented a car and driven it back close to the city. He knew of a large quarry that was currently not in use. It had filled with water and was unusable for the time being. He parked his car at the local rail station that was within walking distance of the flooded quarry. He took the train back into town and called Rickert, asking him to pick him up at the station.

Rickert, although taken aback by the request from someone who had stabbed him in the back, but being a "nice guy," agreed and went to the central station to pick him up. He met Meecham in the underground parking lot, but as they were leaving, Meecham asked him to pull over for a moment. Rickert didn't know why, but being an agreeable guy, he pulled over.

That was when Meecham tazed him; not once, but twice. He then went around, pushed Rickert aside, and took the wheel. He drove Rickert and his car to the quarry, tazed Rickert one more time. Got out of the car, put a stick on the accelerator and sent the car and Rickert over the edge and down into the flooded quarry to disappear into the murky water.

Meecham then picked up the rented car, drove back to the small city he had gone to for work, turned it back in, and took the train home. Not long after, Rickert's wife called Meecham to ask if he'd seen Jerry. Meecham could tell she was broken-hearted and drove to the house to console her. And that's when their relationship began.

I couldn't help but think how cold-blooded and organized the murderer was to plan and execute such a horrendous scheme. I also thought Rickert a trifle anal to provide such a detailed account of his own murder in such chilling detail. Just listening to the brutal details was unsettling. Even Fitz seemed over-whelmed.

Rickert's story got to me, and I decided that I just had to help him and get a cold-blooded killer off the streets. The problem was, I didn't know how I was going to do it. I didn't even know where to start.

19

Chap. 19. Catching a Killer

Wanting to help bring Rickert's murderer to justice and doing it were two different things. I had to do something to at least look like I could help. A good start would be to check out this guy, the killer, and maybe follow him around to see if he would do anything to reveal himself. It was kind of a scary prospect considering the ruthless and brutal murder of Rickert, who may not have been the first. As worrisome as it was, after listening to Rickert's story, I promised I would do everything I could to bring this guy in. A promise is a promise, so when Rickert stuck around after telling about his murder, I asked where I could find this killer.

Rickert felt that his killer, this Fred Meecham fellow, would be spending time with Rickert's wife, probably at his, well, actually, her house. He gave me the address, and, for someone whose material life was over, incredibly detailed instructions on how to get there. If the guy was this obsessive in death, how must he have been in life? Still, it was not a justifiable reason to kill him.

With the details Rickert gave me on how to get to his house, I figured I would take a drive there and see if I could get a look at this cold-blooded assassin. So, Saturday morning, I took a rare car trip into the city to check out the house he was sending me to and to see who might be hanging around. It was a beautiful sunny day and although it had snowed a little last night; the roads were empty. Usually, I commute to the city by train as I have mentioned several times already, but then I was going directly downtown and not tooling around the suburbs.

As I made my way through the streets of what was a higher end neighborhood, Rickert made several random appearances during which he badgered me with renditions of invective and vitriol for his despised killer. It would amaze you just how many ways and with what variety of invective one could say, "I hate that guy. He stole my life, he stole my wife, he took my job, he uses my house."

It was enough ways that I finally had to tell him to either get lost or shut up. He continued his random coming and going, directing me to turn right or go left, naming the streets I should turn on, but mostly bristling so intensely, I could almost hear it. At least he had stopped the clamorous diatribes. Sometimes I amaze myself with my vocabulary, but it truly summed up the ride through the city with the spirit of Jerry Rickert, who had an interesting vocabulary of his own.

When we reached the house, a pulled over to the side of the road, and I have to say, had a sense of awe at the sight of the house. Although I was only looking at the front, I knew it was well above my pay grade now and likely ever. It was a large brick and stucco structure fronted by a large portico. It was kinds like a miniature version of an old style museum or library. I almost expected to see statues of lions guarding the door. Two fir trees, one to either side of the porch columns, were dressed in a slight skiff of snow that set off the leaded panes of the windows. The one on the left being a large picture window, the smaller one on the right with its stained glass could be a reception, or an office or a bathroom. I understood how Rickert could be so jealous.

The lawn was hedged along the sides, but open in front. A small, fenced off area along the walls beneath the windows suggested a well plotted summer floral display. A quick scan of the surrounding homes made it clear this wasn't just any old neighborhood, but one that shouted elegance and old money. After sitting for some time, the wonder faded. Rickert left me to watch, and I did, but nothing happened. There was no movement on the street, and no one stepped out of any door. The place I was watching had become another big house in a neighborhood of big houses. I was about ready to leave when Rickert appeared beside me. "Hold on," he said, "Don't go yet. He's about to come out."

That was my version. Rickert's version substituted 'he' with a much more descriptive set of invectives. As he spoke, the killer stepped out the door. And there was Rickert right beside him, swinging his clenched fists and shouting as he tried to hit him. Of course, it was to no avail. The only one privy to the brouhaha was me and let me tell you, had Rickert been able to land any of the kicks or punches he threw, this Meecham guy would be down and out. The vicious attack and the violent language were so intense, it seemed to me Meecham should have felt some of it. Rickert knew more vicious and profound obscenities than I ever knew existed. It would make a longshoreman blush, hell he might break into tears.

Meecham didn't notice. He walked calmly down the walkway to the street, his head down. He was wearing a tan hip length coat with a fur collar and matching scarf. His chinos were khaki, ending in, my lord; were those galoshes? He had pale blond, receding hair and was hat-less. Beneath his steel-rimmed glasses, his face was clean shaven. He had a mild expression and to my eyes was looking very unmurderly, if that's a word. What's more, his aura showed the pale blue tendrils of someone who was mild-mannered, almost timid. His expression revealed no sign of the darker nature of a cold-blooded killer. Of course, that might be how he looked today after visiting the late Jerry Rickert's wife. It might show differently when confronting a despised adversary. I didn't know that much about the auras I saw.

He walked over to the car parked just behind mine, seemed to look at the gap between the two vehicles, and came to my window and knocked. I rolled it down and in an apologetic tone he stammers, "Sorry, I wonder if you could pull ahead a little bit. I seemed to be hemmed in," and his aura remained unwaveringly pale blue. I smiled and nodded and pulled forward.

"Thank you," he said as he walked back to his car.

Moments later, he had started it and pulled out onto the street. As he passed me, he nodded in my direction and gave a discreet wave. I learned little there, except this guy was either incredibly disciplined, or I was missing something.

20

Chap. 20. Found a Friend

I may have had my first encounter with Rickert's killer, but still had no way to legitimately track down the submerged remains of the late Jerry Rickert and bring his murderer to justice. What's more, I didn't have the remotest idea how I was going to. As far as I was concerned, I had hit a wall, and it bothered me. I was feeling I had nowhere to turn with this. Rickert's murderer would get away with it. Then I realized that wasn't true. I had an ally in the police force.

I broke down and reluctantly called Detective Wenstead. She was more considerate than I expected when I asked if we could meet. She told me she was off duty for the next few days, and we could meet up at the coffee shop again. I told her that would be fine. I worked nearby and could take an early lunch and meet her there tomorrow if it was alright with her. She agreed, and I was about to have my second date with the police, but not the scary kind. The thought of telling any other cop what I knew about Rickert and Meecham sent a shiver through me.

Lucky for me, they didn't put a tight rein on me at work. All they asked, at least in my department, if we did our job and met our deadlines, no one would stand over us to keep us at our desks. I rarely took advantage of this, but sometimes, especially now, with my unwanted but inescapable second career, I did. No one had made a complaint. So, I cut out a bit early for lunch to get to the coffee shop. I wouldn't say I was that eager to meet the detective, but I wouldn't say I wasn't either.

At the counter, I ordered a sandwich and two large coffees. As I made my way to an open table, my silent, well, not quite, partner informed me with an annoyingly knowing grin, "Your good looking police person is about to come through the door."

The moment she came through the doors, her eyes narrowed, and she quickly scanned the room. Seeing me, she gave a slight, ever so slight smile. I waved her over and offered her the coffee I had bought for her. She thanked me and with a soft, "right back," she went to the condiments stand for cream and maybe sugar. I didn't really watch her.

Well, I did, but even with my new and improved vision, as Dr. Dabra had pointed out, I couldn't tell for sure. Perhaps I wasn't looking that closely. I might have been a touch distracted by her casual appearance. Well, Fitz was right, she was attractive, and her blue jeans and burgundy vest over what looked like a very expensive white blouse was very unpolice-like. She looked as if she'd fit in with most of the people I knew, except perhaps for her amber aura with its orange tendrils. I didn't know what it meant. I hadn't seen one quite like it anywhere.

I was still lost in my reverie when she sat down at the table across from me, "Thanks for the coffee," she grinned as she took a sip. "Whew," she said, gasping, "still pretty hot. You must have just got here."

"That's why you're a detective and I'm a small time copywriter who gets pushed around by dead people."

Fritz groaned behind me. The detective looked up sharply at the sound. "Someone here," she asked, "some living spirit, cause, remember, you aren't supposed to call them dead people."

"My bad," I said.

I looked down at the table. There was a kind of stylized floral pattern in a brownish red color. I preferred studying that rather than look at her mocking smile. I know, I know, she wasn't mocking me. It was just me being anxious. "It's my living spirit, job finder, Fitz," I mumbled.

She took another sip of coffee. "Oh, this is good," she said, ignoring my nervous response. Putting the cup down, she leaned across the table and looked me straight in the eyes, "so what's up, Brendan Bannon?"

I explained my dilemma, to which she responded, "Let me get this straight. You've checked the potential killer out, and something doesn't compute. You may or may not know where the body is... because, no matter what your living spirit of Jerry Rickert tells you, you haven't been able to check it out. That it?"

That was so it. "So, what do I do, detective?"

She glanced around as if mention of her detectiveness (is that a word?) bothered her. "Call me, Jenny," she said, "right now, I am a civilian who has some contact with, as you term them, the living spirits of dead people, speaking to someone else with a similar, shall we call it, issue."

"That's what I've been trying to tell him," said Fitz, who was sitting right beside me all that time.

The detective, Jenny's eyes widened, "What's that?"

"That," I said, "is my departed friend Fitz. He's the one who started me off on this whole crazy thing."

"Hi Fitz," she smiled, and I have to tell you it was one hell of a winning smile. "Glad to meet you, or whatever this is."

"The honor is all mine," said a very pleased Fitz, and I could see from his expression that he was sincere. "I don't get to speak to too many of the living except for Brendan here."

I expected a witty comment about me, but she surprised me as she continued to gaze past me and asked, "what about the other spirits?"

"They come and go and it's hard to pin them down. Most of them have something on their mind so they aren't likely to socialize."

"So," she said, "How about Brendan? You spend much time with him?"

"When he needs me. I owe him a lot. He got me out of a tight situation, literally."

"Tell me about it," she said, turning to face me, coffee cup in hand and elbow resting on the table.

Before I knew it, we were deep in conversation about discovering our specialized vision and how we used it. Jenny was good at finding missing persons who, for one reason or another, had died after disappearing. She also liked movies and even played a few of the more popular video games. I was totally amazed to learn her tastes were surprisingly similar to mine. That was when I noticed the place was emptying. I looked at the clock on the wall behind the counter. "Wow," I couldn't believe it, "Look at what time it is. I've gotta get back to work."

She looked at her watch. "We've been talking for over an hour. I guess we were having fun."

Yes, the time flew, and it had been fun. As I got up, I realized that despite the pleasant chat, I had gotten no help. As I stood up to gather the plates and cups to drop them off at the counter, I had to repeat my question from much earlier in the conversation,

"So what do I do?"

Walking with me to the counter to drop off the crockery and toss the trash, she stopped and looked straight at me. "Where do you work, Brendan?"

I told her I worked for InterGlobal Insurance and that I was a copywriter. "Hmmm," and she looked off to her left as she was thinking, "Now," she said, "I'm speaking as Jenny Wenstead, a friend. Your company has an investigative division, doesn't it? They likely carry ID so that when a claim is in question, they can do some interviews. I'm just saying. As a friend. If you do anything, please don't mention my name."

She told me something I hadn't thought about, but she was bang on. As we left the coffee shop and headed our separate ways, I thanked her. "I enjoyed our conversation," she said, "So, please keep in touch and let me know how things go," and she turned away, giving a slight wave as she went.

As I watched her walk off, I had to admit the conversation was pleasant, and I already wanted to do it again. It was an enjoyable lunch, and she had given me a great idea to boot. I raced back to the office and not because I would be late.

21

Chap. 21. Investigations

Jenny, that's what she said to call her. Makes sense. It's her name. Jenny said little about what I might do to move the investigation forward, but she didn't need to say much to give me an idea. I could hardly wait to get back to the office and get started. Was so impatient to get at to, I was bouncing at the elevator and was almost skipping as I entered my work area. At the moment, there was no one in the surrounding cubicles, no surprise for a Monday. Some would be in one of their planning rooms working on a project, some others would be in the international languages section, working on a script for a PR presentation in Mexico. Others would be finishing their last drink at a nearby restaurant. I love working in the creative department.

I ducked into my cubicle and grabbed a couple of poster roughs had been working on and jogged back to the elevator and down to the basement where the large copier was situated and, conveniently, the investigations office. I put my posters down beside the copier and ducked next door to the investigator's room. "Hey Brandon," shouted a friend from the office softball team, Dan Muzinski one of the two investigators in the office, "what's happening.?"

The company had four investigators. Dan was one of them. The other one in the office was someone I only knew as Jim. "I was doing some copying, and I thought I'd drop in and see if anyone was here. Say hi, ya know."

I may be a copywriter, but I'm no master wordsmith. As you can tell by my clever greeting. Fortunately, these guys were fraud investigators, not literary analysts. We chatted briefly, mainly about the softball team and how we would be starting spring training in a little over a month. I wasn't even over Christmas and New Years, although; it had amounted to a lot of nothing. Turkey and gift exchange with the folks, and a few drinks, and paper horn blowing with some single and unattached hockey teammates and, boom! It was time for spring training.

I wasn't going to tell Dan I likely wouldn't play this year but then decided I couldn't pass one of the few good lines I've dreamed up, so I grinned and said, "You know, Dan there's the ghost of a chance I won't be playing this year."

It sounded better in my head. "Crap," Dan smirked, "now who'll we get to carry the bat bag."

So, Dan, one, Brandon, zero. Changing the subject, I asked, "Where are the other guys?"

"Frankie's downtown at the courthouse. Some legal crap about a policy. And Doug, he gone.... Actually, he left yesterday. Got a better-paying job with a detective agency. I think they do divorces. So, if you're tired of playing with the paint boxes and the artsy girls, you could bid for his job."

"Not much play in my department," I smiled, "The only artsy girl who isn't in a committed relationship is a lesbian."

The people in my department were, in fact, great people and

I had a lot of fun there, but it was more like elastic band fights over the cubicle walls than anything more intimate. I would not tell him that. Dan and Jim both stood up, each of them shuffling some papers on their desk in a 'get outa here' maneuver. "Sorry, Bren," said Dan, "we were just on our way to lunch."

Before I could react, they had their coats on and were out the door. "Catch you later," said Dan; Jim gave me a salute.

I followed them through the door to the copy room and waited there until the elevator doors closed behind them. Knowing Dan, lunch would be a long, wet one. Perfect for me. I went back to the investigations office and over to the hook on the wall of the now private eye, Doug Snedden's former cubicle, where his company ID hung from a nail by its neck chain. I lifted it from the hook and brought it back with me to the copy room, where I made several copies of both sides. I folded them and put them in my pocket and returned the ID to its place in Doug's old cubicle.

A while back, when I wasn't sure where I was going to go with the Field Service and Ad department, the firm had offered a course on Photoshop. I hadn't thought too much about it. Now, I was glad I took it, because that night at home, I was able to make a pretty good looking copy only with my name and picture. I balanced the colors, so they matched and only slightly fudged the corporate logo. A legally pointless form of self-protection, I'm sure, but it made me feel better. It didn't specifically identify me as an investigator for InterGlobal Insurance Company, if anyone should ask.

I did the finishing touches at work, and I have to say it looked damned good. Meanwhile, I had dug out a dark gray suit and garish red, blue and orange tie from my graduation and early job hunting days. I set it out, ready to wear. I left work a little early and made my way home to get that suit on. The blue shirt and eye shattering tie along with the gray suit and black walking shoes made me look like a fictional private eye from some not very funny b comedy movie, but with the ID clipped to the breast pocket, I was good to go.

I drove back to the city and followed Rickert's earlier instructions to make my way to the house he said was his and his wife's home. In the fading light, the house looked slightly ominous. I rang the doorbell and moments later, the door opened. The woman at the door was a quite attractive blue-eyed blond, late thirties or early forties, fit and dressed in yoga pants and an over-sized sweatshirt. There was neither question nor threat in her tone as she mildly asked, "May I help you?"

"Trophy wife," was the thought that came to my mind, but I brushed it aside and began my spiel, "Oh, hello," I said, "I'm looking for a Mrs. Rickert, wife of a Jerry Rickert."

She hid a grin behind her hand as if I had stepped on an in-joke only she knew. "Well," she smiled sweetly, "I guess you could say that was me. What would you like?"

"Well," I said, "I work for InterGlobal Insurance, and I'd like to ask you a few questions about your husband."

"Ex-husband," she said, "We've been divorced for some time now. But, come in and I'll try to answer your questions."

She led me through an entrance way to a small sitting room. I had never seen so much polished wood in one place. I had to sit on the edge of the chair she sent me to for fear that I would sink back into its luxurious cushions and disappear. "Would you like some tea?"

I thanked her and declined. "So," she said, as she sat on the plush settee across from me, "what would you like to know about that creep?"

It turns out she was indeed a trophy wife. Jerry had made so many promises when he asked to marry her; none of which he followed through on. In fact, the house we were in was hers, not his. She had made a lot of money as a professional model and actress and already lived in the house when she married Jerry. "After that," she explained, "Jerry moved in, and it was all downhill."

Whatever Jerry was involved in, the home became his drop off spot. It seemed she rarely ever saw him around, and when she did, he was bossy and overbearing and incredibly jealous. She had to give up all her friends, meaning most nights she was home alone with her TV. When she discovered he was having an affair, she confronted him, and he had a meltdown that ended up with the police being called and her demanding a divorce.

"I'm Amy Meecham now, and I couldn't be happier. I know if Jerry had insurance with your company, I would not be the beneficiary. That's fine with me. I want nothing to do with that prick."

According to her, Jerry had been out of her life for some time, but back when they were together, she went to a couple of events with him, where she met Fred Meecham. "He was," she told me with unmistakable glee, "everything that Jerry was not. He was decent, caring, and always a gentleman. When Jerry disappeared after signing the writ of divorce, I turned to Fred. He never pushed me. I guess you could say I pushed him. We've been married for nearly a year now, and I have never been so happy. Is there anything else you would like to know?"

I was going to say no, but then asked, "Do you think he could have been murdered?"

"It wouldn't surprise me. Some of those creeps he hung around could have done anything. He was not a nice man, and neither were most of his associates."

22

Chap. 22. Dead Reckoning

I was able to track down the office where Fred Meecham and Jerry Rickert worked in together. It was some sort of stock brokerage company. Fred wasn't around, and no one had seen Jerry for about a year. I could tell when I asked them. None of his co-workers missed him. Unlike Amy Meecham, the gentlest term I heard from any of them referring to Rickert was, "prick." Most used far more descriptive terms. They agreed with Amy that Rickert was not a nice man. He was a liar and a cheat.

When I questioned them about Meecham stealing his promotion, they all laughed. As one of them said, "Rickert couldn't hold a candle to Meechan. Meecham was smarter, a straight shooter, and everyone liked him. Rickert was lazy and did everything he could to avoid the hard work. Even his co-workers considered those clients he spent the most time with to be particularly shady. This included those co-workers who were willing to admit their own business was questionable. Furthermore, Meecham, had been with the firm far longer than Rickert and had always been next in line for that promotion."

Rickert still went around telling everyone that Meecham had

stolen the job from him, but instead of focusing on work and improving his status with the company, he was almost never around. One of his co-workers explained that Rickert, Meecham, and the others spent time with clients. Rickert seemed to spend a lot more time out than Meecham, however. "This business borders on shady at the best of times," he said, "but from what I could tell, Rickert was underground. When he disappeared, no one really cared. Hell, I thought one of those guys had killed him, or maybe he had killed a client and was on the run. The only thing decent about that guy was his wife, and I am so glad she found her way to Meecham."

I was getting a different picture of Jerry Rickert. Now it was time to complete the picture by checking out the quarry where Rickert said Meecham had dumped him and his car.

The air felt balmy, and the sky was clear and sunny as I set off to find the apparent final resting place of one Jerry Rickert. There had been a warming trend over the last few days, but the countryside was a dreamlike contrast with sunlight reflecting off the melting snow against the dark backdrop of trees and other structures. I had been driving for some time and was quickly nearing the quarry Rickert had located for me the last time he appeared. I was quite close to the site when my phone rang. Actually, it didn't ring; it was Bart Simpson telling me to answer the phone, so I pulled off to the side of the road and did. I recognized the voice immediately, "Brandon?" she said, "Jenny Wenstead here."

"Oh, hi, Jenny," I could be so cool when I got unexpected phone calls from attractive women.

"Sorry to bother you, but I just got word there is some police activity at what might be the quarry you said Rickert told you about. Seems they found a car. You may want to get out there."

"The fact is," I laughed, "I'm nearly there. Been driving around all morning."

"Well," she said, "That's quite the coincidence."

"Yes," I agreed, but I thought maybe it was not all that much of a coincidence. I mentioned Dean Koontz's character, Odd Thomas, earlier. Perhaps, like with him, this wasn't exactly coincidental.

I pulled back on the road and within minutes was at the entrance-way to said quarry. Jenny was right, there was quite a bit of police activity as well as a variety of hard hats, some milling around, others looking more involved. On one side of the quarry, a large crane was slowly raising a coffee-colored Mercedes from the murky mix of muck and water at the bottom. I didn't see that at first, but I took the word of a construction supervisor who was standing around when I walked up to the quarry gate. "I saw all the activity," I said, "What's up?"

"And, who are you, sir?" the guy in the white hard hat asked.

"Nobody, really," I replied, "Brendan Bannon, stringer for the Oshaville Inquirer. Happened to be passing by when I saw the police cars. Since I only get paid for what I submit, I've developed quite an interest in gatherings of police officers. You know, 'all the news that's fit to print' and even some that isn't. But a buck's a buck. So, what's up?"

"Doubt you're going to make much with this one," he said, waving his gloved hand toward the big hole in the ground, "This place has been shut down for years, until someone at the company office reclaimed it about a month back. The quarry was flooded, so we began the process of draining it and that's when we found the car, and from the looks of it, the driver, too, half buried in the muck."

Like the ever eager reporter I pretended to be, I asked, "Do they think the guy was murdered?"

"Are you kidding," he laughed, "that guy had to have been hitting 80 at the gate, and still accelerating to land that far from the edge. For whatever reason he wanted to kill himself, he was in a damn hurry to do it."

"Could someone have jammed the accelerator and sent him off?" I asked.

"Not a chance," said the white hat, "Anybody tried that, it would drag them along with him and over before they could get free. No sir, that guy did it all on his lonesome."

He joined me as I walked over to the edge of the dig, and I could see the car, hooked and being lifted by the crane, was smack dab in the middle of the enormous hole. "If someone jammed the gas pedal, he would have hit the edge at around 30 and dropped over the side." he explained, looking over at the car swinging on the cable from the crane, "He had to be going way faster to get that far."

At that moment, another white hat standing beside a cop called him to come. "Sorry to rain on your parade," he said over his shoulder as he walked away to join them.

I went back to my car and headed home. Something just wasn't computing here. If that was Rickert, and I'm positive it was. I had seen the green glow coming off the car as it was being lifted clear of the mud. A sure sign I had found the body I was looking for, according to Doc Dabra. That meant he killed himself. By now, the knowledge Meecham wasn't a murderer was no surprise, but what was troubling is why Rickert, a dead man, would go about trying to get a living Fred Meecham arrested. What was the message here? Jealousy and hatred could linger on with incredible intensity after death.

23

Chap. 23. Evil Dead

I had to talk this over with someone. Fitz was always available, but Jenny Wenstead, with her police training and her cool observational perspective, would be better. I called her as soon as I got home. She must have been at work, or on a case, because she told me she couldn't talk at the moment, but she'd be home in an hour, and I should call her then. Rickert had been mercifully absent for a few days now, and I was praying he wouldn't show up while I was waiting for a chance to talk to Jenny.

Since Rickert knew I was on the case for him, he had made none of his random arrivals. In retrospect, it might not have been the reason at all. However, this evening, his ongoing absence remained intact. I called Jenny and outlined the complete story. Her response matched my own, although I sensed a smugness in her tone when she reminded me, he was a missing person's case, and the right people were on it. We agreed Rickert was not murdered but had killed himself, and yet, he had employed me to entrap and punish Fred Meecham. Fred, who it turns out was exactly what he seemed, a decent human being.

Still, there was the question of why Rickert did what he did, contrived a scenario intended to destroy Meecham and, as it turns out, his former wife. Neither of us expected he would provide an understandable answer. Jenny suggested I confront him. I wasn't so sure. I was hesitant, because I had seen Rickert in action with Meecham. The significant difference being he couldn't harm Meecham, but he might hurt me. I told you earlier I not only see those living spirits, but they felt as solid to me as any living person. One way or another, I would have to face him. I could wait until he decided on his own to show up, or I could call for him.

It was probably better to get through it quickly, so I called for Fitz. He appeared immediately. I explained what I had learned and asked him if he could find Rickert and get him here. "You really sure you want to see him," asked Fitz, adding, "That fellow scares me."

Yeah, he scared me, too, but I would rather have him show up while I was at home and ready for him, than to have him suddenly appear in some random circumstance like at work, or on the train, or with friends. Me being beaten up by the invisible man would be pretty damn odd to watch, but not as hard as it would be to explain, assuming I would be in any condition to even try.

Fitz vanished, and for a time I was alone. You've probably figured out by now that I am a bit of a nervous Nellie. To my friends, I seem outgoing, but I've always been a bit shy. It was never enough to hold me down, except in some interactions with others. Certain people simply scared me; not a lot, but enough. I sat on my recliner and put on some calming music, trying my best to relax. I was shaking inside, worrying about how I would confront Rickert and how he would respond. Minutes passed extending into a long, dragged out hour when he appeared, already seated in the sofa across from me.

Fitz was there too. I could see him out of the corner of my eye, leaning against the wall beside the hallway to the bedroom. His expression was strained, looking as nervous on the outside as I felt on the inside. "So," said Rickert, and I swear he was giggling with some kind of pent-up glee, "You've got the guy. How did you do it? Where's he going to end up?"

His words came out in a jumble as he strung together a list of questions. Then he stopped. His grin was nothing short of sardonic as he gazed at me across the coffee table. Despite my reluctance, sometimes you just have to say it, and so I did. "Yeah, I found your killer, but I'm still trying to figure out why he did it."

"'Cause he hated me," said Rickert, "he wanted to take over everything that belonged to me. Whatever he gets, he deserves."

"Actually," I attempted a smile, but I could feel it was a no go, "The killer was the guy who slammed on the gas as he entered the quarry and sped over the edge into the water-filled pit below."

"Yeah," chirped Rickert, an eager look on his face, "And it was...?"

"You," I said, "You killed yourself and tried to turn it on Meecham. Your wife had already divorced you, and Meecham was everything you hated. I don't know why you did it, but all the evidence points to the fact you did."

He didn't wait to hear any more. He stood up, walked through the coffee table separating us, and stood over me. There was a terrifying look of hatred in his eyes. And then it began, a rain of invective unlike anything I had heard from anyone that close to my face ever before. He threw a punch at me and ghost or no; it had me reeling backward and seeing stars.

Fitz chose that moment to move between me and Rickert, taking the brunt of his attack. I could not have been more grateful. Rickert stopped his invective and his physical attack, and a split second later he was at my kitchen counter, trying to grab a knife from the block my mom had bought me as a housewarming gift. He couldn't get it, but to my horror, it moved enough to come loose and fall to the table. He came back to look past Fitz, still standing as my defender, and I swear his eyes were flashing red as he looked directly at me and snarled, "I'll get you for this! You just wait," and he was gone.

"You OK boss," asked a solicitous Fitz, "you know you're bleeding."

I wiped the back of my hand across my face and looked at the smear of blood on it, "Well," I was still shaking, but forced a smile, "that went well. I expected I'd be headed to the hospital."

"I don't think he's done with you yet, boss," I could hear a quiver merge with the concern in Fitz's voice.

Had we not seen and, in my case, experienced it with our own eyes, neither me, the living and Fitz, the living spirit, would have believed it possible; he had moved the knife. Fitz strode over to the table and tried to pick the knife up, but his fingers passed right through it. "I don't know how he did that," he said through clenched teeth, "but if he can affect the material world, he could be extremely dangerous."

One more thing for me to worry about. Could the dead effect the living? If a ghost could move something like a knife, could he hone his ability and eventually learn how to wield it against someone who is alive... like me?

24

Chap. 24. Kwick Again

I had learned more about Dr. Dabra's "living spirits" than I had ever wanted to know in those few minutes confronting Rickert. I had thought of Meecham as being brutal and coldly efficient when he was a prime suspect for murder. Now that I knew the truth, I recognized Rickert was the brutal and coldly organized one. He was a living spirit, a ghost, but had physically affected the world of the living when he tried to pull the knife from the block. Yes, he couldn't actually grasp it, and only succeeded in loosening it from the block so that it fell to the table, but until that moment, I was happily convinced that except for me, most were safe from danger at the hands of a supposed phantom such as Rickert.

The incident with the knife, as minimal as it was, sent shivers through me. If a nasty ghost could affect the material world in even the slightest way, it would be elevated from frightening to downright dangerous. Jenny had to know and as soon as I could calm myself, I called her.

She answered the phone with that crisp, business like greeting I referred to as her cop voice. As soon as she knew it was me, her tone relaxed, "So, Brendan, how did it go with our suicidal specter?"

I had to be honest, "not well."

"How do you mean?" she wanted to know.

I then explained the anger, the flashing red eyes, and the physical response of the knife to the living spirit of Rickert's attempt to grab it. This was met by silence on her part. I could almost sense the gears turning in her mind as she mulled over the significance of this. When she finally spoke, her misgivings were clear. "This could be a terrible thing, Brendan. You're right, even a tiny disturbance of the material world by a disembodied spirit could be disastrous. But," and she paused again, "If a malevolent spirit could even control something like a knife, the consequences could be dire."

"And," I added, "if Rickert's post-mortem behavior is any indication, we can be sure there is more than one malevolent spirit around."

This was pause for thought, for sure. Especially for me since I would know of their presence and, most likely, they would know of mine. I expect no one living or dead likes witnesses, especially when they are up to no good; like making me a prime target. Rickert had told me he wasn't finished with me, and I believed him. He was vengeful and, to my mind, downright fiendish. What was more worrisome, he was not alone. I had never thought myself to be particularly alert or wary. I would now have to attempt to pay more attention to the world around me and be ready.

If Rickert had been dead for barely a year and could do that, I wondered, perhaps having seen too many horror shows, if there were others whose malevolence dwarfed his. Evil creatures still existing on this plane of existence, angry, vengeful and destructive. I hated to admit it, but I need Doc Dabra, or someone like him, to advise me. Jenny felt the same way. Problem was, how did we contact him.

Over the next few days, I tried desperately to track him down. The location Jenny had visited differed from the one in the city and the one in my town that I had visited. I talked to as many of the shopkeepers as I could that had been on either side of where Kwick Optometry had been. They never heard of Kwick Optometry or Doc Dabra, and from the look at the neighboring shops, there was nothing to suggest such a place could even have existed. I was able to track down the property landlords. They did not know who or what I was talking about. Jenny told me her results were the same, even when she flashed her badge.

It seems that no one other than Jenny or me had ever even seen a Kwick Optometry storefront, let alone Doc Dabra or his receptionist. No surprise, there was nothing distinctive about either of them. Yet Jenny and I both agreed we could easily identify them anywhere, even pick them out of a crowd. I guess you could say that for us; they were remarkable in a very unremarkable way.

Life's paths can be mysterious., especially for me. I never dreamed such things as ghost, or living spirits as Doc Dabra termed them, existed. Except for the occasional horror movie, I never even thought about them. For me to suddenly see, hear and touch them, to have one show up at my side with the whisper of his name, was still beyond belief. It was beyond belief, but horribly true. I didn't expect this, nor did I expect the flier that appeared in my mailbox the evening after being threatened by Rickert.

Returning from work, I always took a moment to check out my mailbox, usually finding one or two direct mail ads. This time, there was only one of those and the flier.

Three others were checking their mailboxes while I was there, and from what I could gather, it was only in my mailbox and only the mailman had the key. No one had seen anyone else nearby handing out fliers, but there it was, neatly folded and securely locked in my mailbox. There was no address on it, and when I unfolded it, it turned out to be a black and white advertisement for Kwick Optometry. It seems Kwick was having a grand opening on Saturday in a small mall near the outskirts of the city. The flier further informed me that, as a current customer, my attendance at the grand opening would be rewarding.

As I entered my apartment, the phone rang. I picked it up. It was Jenny telling me she had just received a flier from Kwick Optometry. I told her I got one, too. We both agreed it was personal. Jenny told me the mall where it was located wasn't far from her place. She would drive over and look.

About forty minutes later, my phone rang again. "There's no sign of Kwick Optometry there, and none of the merchants I talked to knew anything about it. In fact, they told me that the shops have been under the same management for at least the past twenty years, and they had heard nothing about any change."

All I could say was, "Well, it's not Saturday, yet Jenny."

"Tomorrow is Friday, Brendan. If someone is planning on opening a shop, don't you think there would be some evidence of this happening. Even tiny storefronts require plenty of preparation before opening."

Somehow this did not surprise me, and I suggested to Jenny that we should wait until Saturday, then go to the mall and see. Since she was off duty Saturday, she agreed. We decided to meet in the parking lot and if Kwick was there, we would go in together.

Jenny might not have been sure it would be there. I was certain that somehow it would.

25

Chap. 25. We Got Trouble

The location where Kwick Optometry was having its grand opening was a small strip mall with about a dozen mom and pop type shops. There was the traditional variety store, the small grocery store, the pharmacy, a restaurant, and several others even more unremarkable. I pulled into the parking lot just before the announced ten o'clock opening. And, sure enough, there it was, a few streamers in the window and a couple of garish posters of men women and children in nineteen sixties attire with equally out-of-date hair styles and eyeglasses reminding me of one of the last Beatles's album covers. Jenny arrived within seconds and pulled up beside me as I was getting out of the car. I shut the car door and waited for her to join me so we could make our entrance together.

I was feeling a little smug as I said, "See, I told you it would be here."

She just nodded and strode toward the door. I hadn't noticed before, but there seemed to be a small crowd outside the door. I thought it might be some early shoppers checking out the grand opening sales prices. That's when I realized they weren't looking at the store windows, they were looking at me. In concert, they began walking towards me and I recognized the one leading them in my direction. It was Rickert. "Crap," I groaned, "Rickert's here, and he has his gang with him."

"Where?" asked Jenny, quickly scanning the parking lot.

"Right in front of us," I pointed toward the store.

They were coming for me; they were a rough-looking lot; their clothes torn and soiled, some of them with ruined faces, and the expressions on their faces chilled me to the bone. No horror movie ever frightened me like this little group did. They said nothing as they approached. I backed away, preparing to run. Jenny wasn't very helpful. She only stated she sensed some sort of presence ahead of her and continued to walk toward them. She would likely have passed right through them. She was OK, but I knew I wasn't safe. I was about to bolt when the door of Kwick Optometry swung open. Out stepped the same nondescript lady from the other stores; the one with straight, grayish blonde hair, excessive eye shadow and bright red lips, wearing a gray cardigan with the emblem of some university or college. She was holding a broom. Before I could react to Rickert and his fellows, she waved the broom and shouted, "Ok boys, that's enough. Get out of here."

Their eyes widened with surprise as they turned towards her, and then, instantly, they were gone. The woman at the door had an enormous smile, "Mr. Bannon, Detective Wenstead, welcome, so glad you could make it."

Did she really think we wouldn't? "Come in, come in, Doc Dabra is waiting inside. He'll be so happy you came," and she stood back to hold the door for us. "Where's Rickert and his cronies?" whispered Jenny, looking around, "I can't sense them anymore."

"They vanished when she came out the door and told them to go."

Still holding the door as I stood back to let Jenny go in, the shop assistant slash nurse/ receptionist smiled broadly, "It's so nice to see both of you again, and together. That's wonderful. Doc Dabra will be so pleased."

As I followed in behind Jenny, I looked at the smiling lady holding the door for me and asked, "How did you do that, make those things leave?"

"Oh," she gave a wide grin, "We can't have the riff-raff hanging around during business hours," and that was all she said.

Nothing had changed inside. It was the same interior from the last two locations I had visited. I wasn't an artistic genius, but if it was a franchise, they should immediately replace their designers with some more imaginative ones, although I suspected this was really the same shop, shabby, but exceptionally mobile.

The receptionist ushered us through the inner door to Doc Dabra's office. Nothing had changed, not even him. "Detective Wenstead, Mr. Bannon, welcome, welcome," he said, reaching out to shake my hand, "I see you took my advice and met up with the detective. I'm so pleased, you will be a wonderful team."

Jenny and I looked at each other. Team! What on earth was he talking about? Before either of us drew enough breath to ask what he meant, he turned to Jenny. "Sit in the chair," he smiled, "we'll take a look."

She sat, and he swung the binocular like device in front of her eyes. "Hmmm, very interesting," was all he said, then indicated for us to change places. He stuck that binocular thing in front of my face and said, gleefully, I must add, "Oh, that is very good. Very good, indeed."

"Could you give us some idea what's going on," asked a concerned Jenny.

"I would be happy to. Take a seat and he pointed to a tattered kitchen chair."

Jenny sat. I was still in the primitive dentist style chair. "We've been able to add some small abilities for each of you to help you on your way. If you see, or sense, an unwanted spirit, or anything of the like and you don't want to deal with it. Which you won't, you can just do this," and he held up his hand palm out, fingers spread in the halt gesture and said in a loud crisp voice, "Leave. They will disappear instantly, and most times will never return."

"I put up my hand, palm out, and say, 'leave' and that will send them away?"

"Really don't need the hand gesture. It's just for emphasis," he said.

"I can just say leave and they'll go?"

"Well," he half shrugged, "you don't have to say 'leave' exactly, 'get lost', or take a hike or shove off, or whatever will do. Just say it like you mean it."

"What good will that do me," asked Jenny, "I really can't see spirits. How can I be sure that I am sending off the right ones?"

"There'll be a bit of guesswork on your part," said Doc Dabra, "but you'll get the hang of it."

"But really," Jenny was being very pragmatic, as befits a police detective, and pressed further. "What use is it if I have to guess about something I can't see."

"Sorry, I guess I didn't make it clear," Doc Dabra shrugged again, "Spirits, you sense, but don't see, however, there are other things out there you and Brendan will both see when nobody else does. You may tell them to go, and most will. Good luck," he said dismissively, "We'll be in touch," and turned away to make notations on a clipboard.

The receptionist gave us a warm smile and waved, "See you, dears."

Jenny and I were more confused than ever. We slipped into the restaurant next door and ordered coffee while we tried to come to terms with the limited briefing we had received. There were things out there besides living spirits, and we could both see them. "Yeah," said Jenny, "And most of them will go away when we tell them to."

"Yeah," I said, "that's good, isn't it?"

"Most might go away... MOST, is what he said. What about the ones that don't?"

26

Chap. 26. See That

After the visit to Kwick, things quieted down for me, while for Jenny... detective Wenstead got busier. With my help, we located and extricated final remains from several uncomfortable burial sites. It wasn't nearly as easy as it sounds. Our goals were specific, mostly cold missing persons cases. Of course, not all were dead, and most were, like Nick in the drainpipe, death by misadventure. To get there, Jenny had a lot of research to do, and then with Fitz, we would discuss the records to figure out which cases we might solve. The homing instinct added to my apparently growing repertoire of skills... unwanted skills, I might add. Have I ever told you these were abilities I really wished someone else had been gifted with? Sorry, As I was saying, with my homing instinct, we found quite a few. Quite a few being around 22 percent of the missing persons' files.

We found a few of the living who were among the missing, but quickly learned they had usually disappeared for a reason, and many were not happy with us when we found them. We respected their desire for anonymity unless, of course, they had committed some sort of crime prior to disappearing. Statute of limitations kept us silent about some of these as well. We closed most of those files too, knowing no-one was ever going to follow up with them.

In two cases, we could not track down the remains of missing persons having suffered a violent death, but with their help found their murderers. Through some inventive manipulations, Jenny was able to make the arrests. Since both murderers ultimately confessed, we were lucky enough not to need to give too many details about how we tracked them down. We also found a third murder victim, but the killer was long dead and comfortably ensconced in a distant cemetery. That was good, because I didn't have to interview the living spirit of the murderer. I didn't enjoy visiting cemeteries.

Don't get me wrong, I no longer had any qualms about talking to the dead, even dead murderers, as I learned the vast majority of them were nowhere near as malevolent as Rickert. I was, however, grateful in this case, because I did my best to avoid any sort of graveyard. It wasn't because I was fearful, or even concerned by the spirits I came across there, it was just most of them were only revenants, residual wisps of the original and all they wanted to do was talk. Even those almost entirely faded would repeat their stories to me, much of it they had forgotten, but nevertheless, they would repeat them to me over and over. There had been times had been swarmed by large numbers of them. When they saw me coming, they rushed to greet me to tell me their endless stories. With no concern about interrupting their fellows, they would chatter on. Many with voices that were fainter than the sound of dried leaves blown by a gentle breeze.

The recently dead were louder and more lucid, but in most cases, their stories were of little interest. Still, they all seemed to share the need to talk to someone living, and I was the only one they could find who might listen.

On the few occasions I had to visit a cemetery, I tried to talk Jenny into joining me, but although she could hear the voices of the recently dead, they were unaware she could, so they left her alone. In my case, there would be twenty or more spirits surrounding me within minutes of my arrival. Some barely visible wisps, some as solid as the living and everything in between. They would harangue me with their endless and often pointless tales, usually an assortment of anecdotes from their past lives. Jenny just thought it was too weird for her and after the first time, refused my invitations.

On a positive note, the number of cold cases we were able to close the book on was considerable. Since Jenny was the formal detective and I officially some sort of unofficial hanger around, the credit went to Jenny. Now, Jenny was always ready to share the credit, but I advised against it. It would be just too odd for a small time corporate copywriter to be good at finding dead people.

Our combined efforts and their success had been good for Jenny's reputation on the police force. They promoted her to detective sergeant assigned to missing persons. While this promotion could only assist us in our work on the missing persons' file, it also added another dimension to the newly minted Detective Sergeant's responsibilities. As Fitz had suggested some time back, even in uniform, she was quite a looker and I believe because of this, became a regular at the division commander's public relations ventures. Whenever the commander or even the chief had a news conference or delivered a formal statement, Jenny was usually somewhere just off center, but still on camera, looking both pretty and efficient in her sergeant's uniform. Although I teased her and told her she was there for her excellent visual effect. I would add she provided an excellent contrast to the bulldog features of the chief. She would blush and insist she was there because it was her and the other officers' jobs to survey any assembly for anyone who appeared in any way suspicious.

We were driving around on Jenny's off day patrol looking for signs of any out of place human remains. It was something we began doing regularly since her promotion. She would use this as an opportunity to fill me in regarding what was happening in the policing world. The things she could share, of course. One morning she didn't seem that interested in driving and suggested we stop for a coffee. As we entered to take a seat, she picked up the front page of a newspaper that had been forgotten at one of the empty tables. She handed it to me, pointing to the front page. "What do you think of that?" She asked.

"What do I think of what?" I answered.

"Look at the main story," she said.

"What?" I said, "another mass shooting?"

"Read it carefully," she ordered.

I did what she told me, and my jaw dropped. Some homeless guy had gone into a building at lunchtime and began shooting. A few people were hurt, no-one seriously before the shooter was wrestled to the ground by security guards except one, an employee on his way out to lunch, a man named Fred Meecham. The shooter, when questioned, had no recollection of any of it. Except, now Fred Meecham was in hospital with critical injuries. What was that all about?

27

Chap. 27, Yeah, Thanks Doc

Meecham in hospital, critically wounded by some homeless shooter. What was it all about? I had to know. Why Meecham? Why a nice and well-respected person like Fred Meecham? In all my investigations, the only one I had ever found who hated Beecham and would willingly have killed him was the late Jerry Rickert.

As we quietly sipped our coffee, I had to ask Jenny what she knew about all this. In her new position within the administration, Jenny did not disappoint. The moment she heard the name Fred Meecham at the office, her ears had perked up. She realized she knew the name and quickly came up with the association. Trying not to be too obvious, she asked some of the participating officers what she hoped were innocent questions., "So," she said, "I asked around in what I would look like idle curiosity to see what I could find out."

"Seems this homeless guy walked into the reception area of Meecham's building when many of the employees were heading off for lunch. The receptionist said that he stood by the elevator doors as if he was waiting for someone. Although he looked pretty disheveled, they let him be. Then suddenly, as one of the elevator doors opened, he started shooting. The first person coming off the elevator was Meecham, and he took the brunt of the attack. The other injuries apparently were because of the wildness of the shooter. Security got to him quickly and were able to take him down and disarm him easily."

"Security told the first police on the scene that once they got the guy down, he gave no resistance. He looked confused and kept asking where he was and why they were holding him. Arresting officers and those questioning him back at the station all agreed the guy really seemed to have no comprehension of why he was arrested or what he had done. He claimed he didn't know where he got a gun or why he was in that building with it. Investigators figured he had to be lying, but they were impressed by his ability to appear innocent and ignorant of any wrongdoing. What do you think that means?" Her eyes narrowed as she looked straight at me over the top of her half raised coffee cup.

I thought a moment, then said, "Perhaps, in some way, he was innocent and ignorant. Perhaps the living spirit of Jerry Rickert got to him somehow. Sounds a touch outlandish, I know."

"Yeah," she forced a grin, "I thought the same damn thing."

"We clearly need Doc Dabra." My laughter as strained as her grin.

"Who knows," she smiled, "Maybe we'll stop out of here to see his shop right in front of us."

When we stepped out, it wasn't right in front of us. It was off at the far end of the shopping center from the coffee shop. "Was that there when we pulled in," Jenny asked, dumbfounded.

I was sure it wasn't. Once seen, the Kwick Optometry shop wasn't some place you would ever easily miss. As we turned towards it, the absolute weirdness taking over my life nearly overwhelmed me, living spirits, supernatural evil, a seedy shop, and its odd occupants showing up all over the place. What I didn't know at the moment was my life was about to get a hell of a lot weirder.

"Mr. Bannon, Detective Sergeant Wenstead, so wonderful to see you," gushed the receptionist, as if our appearance was a total surprise, "I will let Doc Dabra know you are here," and she stepped through the door into his office slash treatment room, or whatever.

"Go right on in, dears. The doctor says he is free at the moment and can see you now."

Who was she kidding? When a shop suddenly shows up when and where you need it. When there is never anyone else inside except for the receptionist and the so-called doctor, how could he possibly not be free to see us right away?

The receptionist held the door for Jenny and me. As the door closed behind us and my eyes were adjusting to the dimness of the room, I could see Doc Dabra was on a telephone. It looked like one of those ancient crank phones, only there was no crank and what he held to his ear wasn't connected to anything.

He was speaking in what seemed a louder than necessary tone. "That's right," He said, "earth, human earth, narga earth, pringon earth, you can name them all if you want, but at the moment it seems confined to the human earth portion of the dimension," he paused as if listening then added, "Yes becoming quite active... no, no small scale at the moment... ok do what you can."

He hung up the earpiece and turned towards us. A huge smile on his face. "Ah," he said in much softer tones, "Detective Wenstead, Mr. Bannon, so good to see you. How can I help.?"

We told him about what had happened to Fred Meecham, explaining our concern about the down and outer who did it. How he claimed he couldn't remember why or where he got the gun. "I believe he was sincere," Jenny added.

The doc looked off to the left and scratched his temple. "Oh dear, I was afraid of that."

"Afraid of what?" queried Jenny.

"To tell the truth, when I first heard Mr. Bannon's story about the living spirit of Mr. Rickert moving the knife, I hoped it was nothing more than a last act before moving on. This happens. It's why there are so many stories of people having a brief contact with their deceased loved one. Usually, it's at the moment of death or at a time of high emotion. However, I suspect this is something else."

Jenny took the words right out of my mouth, "What do you think it is?"

To be honest, she asked it before I had even gotten my head around ghostly contact with loved ones. As befitting a doctor of something or other, Doc Dabra gave us a very technical explanation of what he believed was happening.

An ancient and evil cult, masters of necromancy, through study and contact with demons, increased their power and control over others, but only when dead. Their power rituals often ended in violent suicide. They could possess people and even draw on their strength and knowledge. Rickert must have learned about this and did some quite remarkable research. The definitive text is the Necromancium. "It's very rare, but if he got his hands on it...." And his voice trailed off.

Dabra concluded his lesson stating, "The fact that he chose a frail homeless person suggests his power to possess is not yet fully developed,"

"He'll get better at it." I blurted.

Dabra just nodded.

"Are we in danger?" asked Jenny.

"We are all in danger," replied Dabra, adding, "there are evil people out there willing to offer their bodies to a demonic spirit in exchange for growing their own evil power."

Jenny turned to face me, "You better watch out, Brendan, Rickert did not like you. You are likely a target."

My spidey sense told me she was on to something, and I should be scared. No problem, there. As we left Kwick, the receptionist, her voice sweet and far too cheerful for my liking, said, "be careful out there, dears."

I felt more like a deer in the headlights.

28

Chap. 28, Add D to Evil

While we were heading to our cars, Doc Dabra's receptionist called to us, "Doc wants you to know the aura of a possessed person will appear red with black at the tip. The brighter it is, the stronger the spirit possessing them."

"Thanks," I called out.

I would have called her by name, but I didn't know it and never have found it out. She waved and gave us a cheery smile before going back into the shop. I turned to Jenny, "Well, that's great. I hardly even notice auras anymore. That's like telling us you'll hear a click just before the bomb goes off."

"The combination of red and black is distinctive," Jenny returned, "at least it's something."

"Are you kidding," I said, "I'll be looking for cover every time I see a billboard or sign with red and black together in the distance."

I think she thought I was joking. She laughed as she got in her car. I was in no mood for humor at the moment.

Turning out of the parking lot behind Jenny, something occurred to me. Something I needed to speak to Jenny about.

I honked my horn, came up beside her and signaled for her to pull over. She did right away. I drove up behind her and stopped, got out of the car, and walked up to her window. She rolled her window down and looked at me with a big grin on her face. "Shouldn't it be me doing the traffic stop," she laughed.

I always make jokes when I'm feeling anxious, so I let it go with a half smile. "What if it is Rickert, and he comes back again to finish the job with Meecham? And what about his ex-wife, Amy? He wasn't too happy with her marrying Fred."

The grin was gone, replaced by a series and thoughtful expression. She was quiet for a moment, then said she see if she could get an officer to keep watch on Fred. Amy would be up to me. "See," she said, "I told you to get a Private Detective license. You're doing the job, anyway."

I stood by my car as she drove off and watched her go. For the moment my mind was blank until someone in a passing car shouted, "Get off the road before you get killed, idiot."

Good advice. I got back into my car and headed home. Looked like Jenny was right. I was about to play private detective, lots of time, zero pay. Bad enough, but I was also a potential target. I must have said something to that effect out loud because a voice from the back seat spoke, "Don't worry, boss, I'll look out for you."

After I got over the momentary shock, I said, "Fitz, where have you been?"

"Here all the time, boss. You haven't talked to me for a while, but," he emphasized, "I'm always watching your back."

"Thanks," I muttered.

"Yeah, boss, I heard what the doc Dabra fella said, and I'm pretty damn sure it was Rickert controlling Meecham's shooter. And, we both know how he feels about you. Frankly, I'd rather you stayed alive. I kinda like this relationship we have. It's like those buddy cop movies you watch on tv, a living guy to cover the streets and a ghost to get into the tight spots."

"I appreciate that," I said, and I did, but had to add, "still, there is something about this Rickert. If he is powerful enough to possess someone who is alive, what might he do to you."

"Good point," he said.

We were both silent for the rest of the trip home.

Once back home, I quickly picked some things I would need and put them in a backpack I hadn't used since college. You know, a flashlight, water, a change of clothes, a box of cookies. "A gun," you ask.

No gun. Don't own a gun. Never shot a gun. Wait, I lie. I had shot a gun. It was at a carnival shooting gallery. Won a littler rubber duck for being the worst shot there.

Not long after gathering my things, I was back on the road heading for the city and the Meecham home where I was hoping to find Amy. Of course, no one was there when I arrived. I had to smack my head.

Where else would she be but at the hospital with Fred?

When I arrived, there was a uniformed police officer seated on a chair beside the door of Fred's room. When it comes to police matters, Jenny seemed able to work miracles. A guard would appear unnecessary for many with the perpetrator in hospital himself, but there he was.

I asked if for her to come see me. He nodded, opened the door and called in, then went back to looking at his phone. Amy came out. "Hi," I said, "I'm Brendan Bannon from the insurance company."

She smiled slightly. "Of course, I recognized you right away, Mr. Bannon. Forgive me if I'm a bit distracted right now. How can I help you?"

"I hope you aren't going to go home tonight," I said.

"No, certainly not. I've been here in this room since they brought him in. I'm not going home till we can go together."

"I understand," I said, adding, "Do you have anywhere to stay if you need to get some rest, or change?"

"Yes, I've booked a room in a nearby hotel. In fact, I was planning to go over there shortly to get a few hours of rest. Fred seems to be doing much better, and I am exhausted."

She gave me the name of the hotel and that's when I told her about my concern for her safety and asked if she would tell the front desk I was her bodyguard. It would let me hang around the lobby for the night. She wasn't sure why I was worried, but she was happy to oblige.

Some time later, me carrying her overnight bag; we walked together to the hotel. She went to her room while I nodded at the desk clerk, picked up a newspaper and found a pleasant corner where I could watch the doors. I called Fitz. He showed up immediately. "Let me know," I whispered, "if you spot someone with a red and black aura."

"Sorry boss," he responded, "I don't see auras."

"Ok," I returned, "then let me know if you notice anyone who looks out of place here."

"No problem, boss, it should be pretty easy."

It was a four-star establishment, and everyone in there looked distinctive enough any outsider would quickly catch your eye.

Early on, I spent most of the time looking over the top of the newspaper. Then I got engrossed in some of the stories. The last thing I remember seeing was the comics.

I don't know how long I dozed before I heard Fitz. "Boss, wake up. There someone here who doesn't seem to belong."

I opened my eyes and there was the red aura tipped with black. The bearer of that aura was at the main desk. I saw the clerk shake his head and then glance my way. He dipped his head to the side in a "come here, I think this guy is for you," sort of motion.

As I made my way over to the man with the distinctive aura wearing a dirty, torn overcoat turned from the desk clerk to look my way. "You," he snarled, and pulled a nasty-looking hunting knife from his coat pocket, holding it like a skewer, he came at me.

29

Chap. 29. Being the Target

Some disheveled street person was about to stab me. Why didn't I expect this? My life didn't flash before my eyes, but rather, my stupidity. Somehow, I thought the possession to be single-minded. Rickert would direct the possessed person like a drone, focused on his prime target, Amy. I never dreamed it would be like he was in there driving and aware enough to take out a secondary target.

This thought was a tiny nugget in a vast cloud of abject fear. Fitz tried to jump in front of my assailant. Naturally, he passed right through him. I put up my arms to deflect the knife and felt the blade against my hand. It deflected away from my thought and caught me just below my right shoulder. It surprised me I didn't feel any pain as I reached to grab his hand. I was holding his wrist as he struggled to pull the blade free. That's when I felt the pain. My eyes seemed to fill with dark clouds. I felt my grip relax on the attacker's wrist.

The pain was so intense; it seemed to take over my entire body. I was sure I was dying. Then everything went dark, and the pain faded away.

Next thing I heard was an unfamiliar voice saying, "It's amazing how little damage the blade caused. Messed up his hand some. I stitched up the slash, deep but fairly clean. Might be a bit of a scar. As for the shoulder. It's going to be really sore for some time but should heal completely."

Another voice spoke. "It's his hand I'm concerned about. Will he lose any function?"

"Doubt it," came the other speaker, "Perhaps a little. If that's the case, we can book some physio."

"How about his head," the second voice asked.

"Hit the arm of the chair pretty hard when he fell, trying to defend himself. Good thing it was cushioned leather. I expect he'll have a headache for a day or two. Nothing serious there. I've given him a shot of painkiller. He'll need to rest for a few hours."

The voices faded out. Then I saw a bright light. "Oh no," I thought, "I'm dead. I'm going into the light."

"I think he's coming around," said another voice that sounded very much like Jenny's.

What was Jenny doing here? Was it heaven or hell or wherever? Then I opened my eyes. I was on a bed in a hospital room. Jenny and Amy Meecham were both there. Amy seated in the armchair, Jenny standing beside the bed looking down at me. She looked quite shaken up, but when she saw my eyes were open, she smiled. It was the most beautiful smile I have ever seen.

"Thank God you're awake," she said, "Rickert nearly got you. Fortunately, the night security was in the lobby when he attacked. He was able to get him off you and hold him down. Other hotel staff got you away and to the hospital."

"Amy," I smiled, but it was a weak one, "I was supposed to protect you."

"Well, as far as I'm concerned, you did," she said, "if you weren't there, chances are, he would have found me. The desk clerk was suspicious. He was not a typical guest or visitor that I might entertain and refused to release the number of my room to him."

"However," she continued, "I've stayed here many times and if Jerry told him where to find me, he would also tell him I preferred the penthouse floor away from any activity. There are only four rooms on the floor and three of them were empty."

I couldn't restrain myself, "that was Jerry. At least he was driving."

"What do you mean," Mrs. Meecham asked abruptly.

Before I could answer, Jenny cut in, "I think we should let him rest a bit longer. He did get quite a bump on the head. At least that's what the doctor said. Let's get a coffee."

Amy Meecham rose gracefully to her feet and joined Jenny at the door to the room. As they stepped to in the hall, I heard Jenny say, "Hang on, I left my phone in the room. Let me get it. I'll be right back."

She ducked back in the room, came close to me and whispered. "I'll take her back to her hotel. You get out of here. There's an all-night restaurant across the street from the main doors. See you there in a half hour or so."

As she left the room, she looked back at me and mouthed, "Move."

Within the half hour, I was out of the hospital and sitting at a booth in the all-night bistro. My head was woozy, but otherwise I felt little pain. My hand tingled and there was a slight aching in my shoulder. I was hoping it would stay that way, but I knew it would hurt like hell when the painkiller wore off. The over-the-counter stuff they prescribed for me would not help much.

The booth was near the front window, so Jenny would have no trouble seeing me. When she arrived, I waved. She saw me and walked over to the table. She was about to sit down when she glanced over at the window.

With a look of alarm, she rushed to me, grabbed my arm. Even the hospital painkiller couldn't mask the effect of her pulling me to my feet. "Run," she intoned, and without releasing her grip pulled me across the floor just as a car crashed through the window, scattering shards of glass and pieces of table and bench. The bench where I had been sitting a moment earlier.

Apart from a wave of gratitude for my fast acting detective friend, I was acutely aware of the driver and his look of aghast bewilderment as the car shuddered to a stop against the fortunately untenanted front counter.

Jenny only paused for a moment to watch the car come to a stop, then said, "Let's get out of here, and fast. Rickert seems to be picking up the possession thing on the fly."

And then, there he was in the living spirit flesh or whatever. His voice cool and controlled, he stated flatly, "Just letting you know. Right now, I have other fish to fry, but soon you will die. You too," he said, turning toward Jenny.

She may not have seen him, but she heard him loud and clear. As fast as he appeared, he was gone. Outside the restaurant, she was pulling me along, flashing her badge, as she hurried down the street to her car.

30

Chap. 30. Tracking Evil

The next few weeks were awful. Basically, I was on the run. I spent a couple of nights on Jenny's sofa, but Fitz told me he had noticed several hobos as he called them, showing up in the neighborhood at different times. They may well have been some random homeless men who got lost and were looking for handouts, but I doubted that.

When I called the office to tell them I wouldn't be in for a few days, the secretary told me street people had come into the building asking about me. Three different ones had approached central on separate occasions, demanding to know where I was. The two ladies who manned that position were understandably frightened. The encounters weren't pleasant. Each was belligerent and insistent, and two of them had to be physically escorted out of the building.

When I called my landlord to hold my mail. He told me my apartment had been ransacked; the door was broken; furniture was smashed, and papers scattered around. Hearing a disturbance from my room and knowing I wasn't there; he called the police. The police found a mentally challenged homeless guy in my bedroom and arrested him. He was staring out the window when they found him and didn't seem to understand who they were and why they were there.

Amy Meecham had gone home from the hospital to find the door kicked open and some of Fred's stuff thrown around. She immediately left to return to the hotel. Amy didn't drive. She had a driver who had driven racing cars and trained police. Thanks to his driving skill, he was able to barely avoid a truck that had swung into his lane. A few minutes later, a car pulled out of the mall against the lights. It seemed intent on hitting them. The driver was able to avoid the full impact, but the result was a messy fender bender. The driver of the other car claimed he didn't know what happened. It was as if someone had taken control of his body, holding his foot on the accelerator when he tried to go for the brake.

Amy wasn't hurt, but like me, she was terrified.

Speaking to her on the phone, all she could say was, "I don't know how, Mr. Bannon, but I think Jerry was responsible."

I guess she was something of a sensitive much as Jenny was, only not as pronounced. The good thing about it was, she was quick to agree her life was at risk and followed my advice to get out of town. She and her driver devised a deception that apparently worked, allowing her to get to the railway station and on a southbound train without incident. How safe she would continue to be was a question, but fortunately, even a living spirit with the powers Rickert was displaying could not be in two different places at the same time. Fortunate for her; not necessarily for me.

Jenny and I decided to go in separate directions. She needed to be available for work, so found places to spend her off time relatively close to home. When she told me about her decision, I informed her I wasn't happy with it. She shrugged and went into her room to gather her uniform and several changes of clothes.

At least she had a gun. To this point, however, most of the possessed seemed innocent enough after the fact. I don't believe she would even consider shooting unless they left her with no choice and... could get it from her holster fast enough.

I'm assuming Rickert still found it difficult to invade and control most people, and he must have run out of the malleable homeless. Things seem to quiet down. After a week or so of running, I decided it was time to return to my apartment. At least, to clean it up. As I lifted the police tape and stepped through the door, the living spirit of Jerry Rickert confronted me. I noticed he was about to say something, and one of my few larger trophies on the counter was shaking.

To my surprise, and no doubt his, I was so pissed at the moment, I shouted at him, "Get the hell out of here, and don't come back."

His eyes widened, and then he was gone. "Bravo, boss," came a voice from behind me, "I don't think he'll be back for a while."

I so hoped Fitz was right, and for some time it seems he was. Things felt back to normal, but I still had my concerns.

Perhaps I would apply for a private investigator's license, as Jenny suggested. For now, I just wanted to get back to work. The next morning found me on the train headed for the city and my office.

It's hard to say what caused me to look at the house where I'd seen the cat and the young, half decomposed young lady who had asked me where I'd been, seemingly so long ago. Since those early days, I had passed by it without a glance. But, this day it drew my eyes. There was no sign of the girl, but the guy with the dark beard wearing the robe who had laughed at me was standing in the backyard. He had a wide smile on his face as he raised his arm and pointed at me. "Cheviot!" I croaked, loud enough to startle some people sitting near me.

If fear were palpable, it would be a dark, dank cloud, and at the moment, such a cloud enveloped me. I knew with no doubt that a terrible evil was coming, and I was on its to do list. I sat unmoving for the rest of the journey, staring across the carriage to an advertisement on the wall near the door to the next car. I don't have the foggiest clue what it was for.

Still in a fog, I trudged up the street from the station. About halfway to the office, I realized someone was calling my name. The cheeriness of the voice seemed completely out of place. I looked around to see Doc Dabra's receptionist waving at me. She was standing in front of; you guessed it, Kwick Optometry. "Doctor Dabra would like to see you for a moment, Mr. Bannon, if you don't mind."

"What the hell," I thought, or words something to that effect, and turned towards the weather-beaten facade and the smiling lady holding open the door.

"Welcome back," she said as I passed her and in the door.

"Thanks," I replied, but my heart wasn't in it.

31

Chap. 31. Chivot

Doc Dabra was standing beside the open door to the back room when I stepped into his shop. Like his receptionist, he smiled. It just wasn't as cheery, and that better suited me. "Come on through," he said, gesturing towards the open door.

As I went in, he added, "How is your hand? I understand it was a deep slash."

I couldn't imagine how he knew about my hand. It didn't surprise me either. Anyone who could move an entire shop from place to place without being noticed would have his ways. The cut had been deep, but was healing well, although slower than I liked. "It's coming along nicely," I answered.

"That's good," he said.

He pointed at the old dentist style chair and told me to sit down. He slid something that looked a bit like a tv table up under my arms. It looked like nothing more than a wide piece of board, painted white with two large Xs drawn on in black. "Could you take your bandage off? I need to check your hand before we proceed."

It didn't seem to make much sense to remove a bandage I had

struggled to put on not that long ago and why an optometrist would want to see my hand was beyond me. However, he was Doc Dabra, so I did what he asked.

The palm of my right hand was still inflamed. A scab had formed over most of it, and it still hurt if I moved it too much. Doc Dabra looked at it carefully, avoiding touching it. I appreciated that. "Yes, it will do," he muttered to himself, then said to me, "OK, Mr. Bannon place your hands palm down on the Xs."

A strange request, but I obliged. The moment the palms of my hand touched the board, I felt intense burning pain. It hurt far worse than the knife wound. I tried to pull my hands away, but they wouldn't move. Then, as quickly as the pain had started, it was gone. My hands actually felt fine. Now I could lift my hands and look at my palms. The only difference I could see was the wound on my right hand was completely healed. There was a barely noticeable scar where the wound had been.

Doc took what looked like a pen out of his pocket and pointed it at my palms. I don't know how, but it revealed two interlocking triangles on each hand forming something that resembled, but wasn't quite pentagrams, with a stylized S running through them.

"Excellent," he again muttered to himself, then looked at me. "How do your hands feel?"

They felt just fine, and I told him so, then asked what those symbols were all about. "I heard you were running into trouble with Rickert and those he possessed. So, I've handed you armaments, if you'll forgive the pun."

"Across from you," he continued, "is a target. Do you see it?"

Of course, I did. It looked like one of those human silhouettes you see in movies when the hero is practicing his shooting.

"Good," he smiled, "face your palms to the target and when you're ready, let go."

I didn't understand what he was talking about, but I did what he asked. For a moment, nothing happened and then, two blue green lightning bolts shot out from my hands, hitting the target and demolishing it. "What was that?" I shouted in amazement and terror.

"That will help you with malevolent spirits and anyone they possessed. It can be very destructive, but you control the impact unconsciously, so don't worry, it won't turn you into a killer."

"Wow," I giggled, "It's like I have a superpower."

His tone was serious as he said, "Don't assume too much from this ability. You are not invincible. Spirits capable of possession are themselves quite powerful. Like you, they will grow into their abilities. Rickert is one. There are others, and he will find them, or," he added ominously, "they will find you."

He ushered me from the room, patted my shoulder, and went back. The receptionist smiled her cheerful smile one more time. "We'll be seeing you, Mr. Bannon," and as I left, added, "you might suggest Detective sergeant Wenstead look for us. She could use a defensive tune up, too."

"I'll let her know," I said.

Back on the street on my way to the office, I turned my hands over to check the symbols on my palms. All I could see was a pencil thin scar on my right hand, a barely noticeable reminder of how close Rickert had come.

Passing a billboard, I thought to try a test shot, but then it occurred to me I really didn't need to be vandalizing property or explaining the fireworks display coming from my car should anyone be watching.

In the office, although none said anything, I could feel their eyes following me as I headed for my desk. The department supervisor approached me to ask how I was feeling and if I had completed the jobs assigned to me. Although he said it didn't worry him, I was a good worker, I could tell he had some concern about my reliability these days. It was a sign to me my time with the company was ending.

The local college was offering a fourteen week class on investigations, techniques and procedures. I signed up and did my best to keep up. In the meantime, Jenny and I continued our investigations into the higher profile cold cases, even solved a couple.

College certificate and Jenny's written reference in hand, I applied for and received my private investigator's permit. My only client at the moment was the city police, and the position was temporary. Detective Sergeant Wenstead could hire me only while on a case requiring research. I was the designated researcher. Having resigned from my copywriting position, I was, for all intents and purposes, jobless.

I did some freelance writing, but contracts were few and far between. Still, the payouts were adequate enough to stock my fridge and have a beer or two at one of the locals. It all made for many hours of doing nothing. Sometimes I would gas up my car and go for a ride.

On one of those drives, I was on a secondary highway close to the New Structure communal compound where the old house I had seen from the train stood. I didn't have any fond memories of my experience there and drove past the turnoff without a sideways glance.

The radio was playing quietly as I drove, so when I heard the words, "Brendan, my boy, we haven't seen you for a while," I thought the station was taking a commercial break.

That is, until I realized it was directed at me personally. Someone was sitting in the passenger seat. Someone who hadn't been there a moment ago. I turned my head to look. It took me a second to recognize it was the bearded guy wearing the robe I had seen laughing at me when I ran out of the crumbling house after encountering the person with the hideously decomposed face. "Really, Brendan, you should come by. I'm sure Tracy would be happy to cook you up a lovely spider and centipede stew," and he laughed, adding, "We get so few visitors these days."

"Chivot," I choked out.

"In the... well, no, not in the flesh, but indeed, it is I, Brother Chivot."

The way he said it, it sounded like Sheev-oh. "You interest me a great deal, Brendan. You could see Tracy, as disfigured as she must have been, to frighten you so, and you saw me. I have some plans and could use a little help from a living visionary. Let me explain."

I was not happy to have this unexpected and uninvited hitch-hiker in my car. I knew his story and wanted nothing to do with him, living or dead.

"Take a hike," I snarled.

An exasperated screech was quickly cut off, and Chivot was no longer present. I hoped Doc Dabra's receptionist was right, and he would be one who didn't return. Despite the hope, I had an uncomfortable sense I was far from finished with Brother Sheev-oh. The thought made me shiver. What really chilled me, however, was how he had known my name.

32

Chap. 32. Rickert Again

Something else to worry about; The living spirit of former cult leader and suicide, Carl Chivot wanted to recruit me. Well, whatever it was he had planned for me, I was not in the least interested. It was bad enough being chased around by Jerry Rickert. I just wanted the lot of those living spirits to just go live their death somewhere far from me. I wanted it, but I couldn't say it out loud, as I had become quite attached to Fitz. As for all the others, disappear... completely!

It might be what I wanted, but I knew it wouldn't happen. I was bound to the world of the dead right from the moment Doc Dabra set me down with the binocular looking tool he had. He wouldn't let me blame him, though. I had the vision already, or so he told me, and he had just brought it into focus, drew my attention to it. Be that as it may, I can tell you I would have been just as happy never to have been focused on, or paying attention to ghosts.

I was back in town heading for home, ruminating about ghosts and Chivot and Rickert and my preference of never having encountered them. Not exactly distracted from my driving, but not particularly concentrating either when Fitz shouted, "Look out!"

From the corner of my eye, I saw a car speeding out of a side street and headed straight for me. I hit the gas and tried to turn away from the oncoming vehicle. It hit me, but fortunately, thanks to Fitz's warning, it wasn't the broadside impact it could have been. Instead, my turn and acceleration reduced the impact, but the collision still sent my car swerving across the road and onto the sidewalk. The left rear of my car had imploded from the force, but I had avoided the worst of it.

I had been thrown around but didn't feel too badly hurt. Hearing a shout from behind me, I turned to see the driver of the other car, a middle-aged man in a business suit, fall out the door of the other car. Engulfed by an aura of red tendrils fringed with black, he stumbled to his feet and came toward me, tire iron in hand. I raised my hands to protect myself from the imminent blow and saw a blue green stream of flame shoot from my palms and strike my attacker. He stopped immediately and dropped the tire iron. The black tipped red aura that had surrounded him vanished. "What the hell happened," I heard him shout as he looked blankly around.

Next thing I knew, he was at my window asking me if I was alright. With a little effort, I was able to open the door and get out. He stood there, looking concerned about me. He should have been more concerned about himself. Blood dripped down from his scalp. His left arm hung limply at his side, and in that instant, he collapsed to the ground. A crowd gathered and someone had called 911.

Within minutes, the police and an ambulance were on the scene. Neither car would be driving away and neither driver would be going anywhere but to the local emergency room. I tried to tell them I was fine, then nearly fell in front of one of the police officers who grabbed me and held me up. I clearly wasn't fine.

After an ambulance ride and a brief visit with the emergency room doctor, I was given a clean bill of health. I had a couple of bruises, and my leg was a little sore from banging the dash, but otherwise I was ok to go. As the old joke goes, "you should see the other guy," and indeed he would spend more time at the hospital under close observation. Not only had the collision been rougher on him and his injuries more damaging, his inability to remember anything about what had happened until he came to my window concerned the medical staff.

I knew why he couldn't remember, but couldn't tell them, or they would keep me for observation, too. Rickert was behind this. I called Jenny to tell her what had happened. The first thing she asked was if I was ok. When I told her I was, her voice relaxed, and she got serious. "You have to be really careful, Brandon. You are far from being out of the woods as long as Rickert hates you and wants to kill you. Maybe more than he wants to kill Amy or Meecham.... "

"Or you," I added softly.

"Or me," she agreed.

"So, what do I do," I asked. "It's impossible to be on guard every moment, and he's getting cagier. He can play it cool with me, or strike at any time. It's bloody terrifying. My life has come down to this, looking over my shoulder constantly."

"Maybe Fitz could help," she suggested. "Perhaps find a few associates to be on the lookout for you."

"I can ask," I said, "and I'm sure he'll help, but you know spirits can't see auras. It's the only sign there is to tell Rickert's around."

"You need some human eyes, too," Jenny said.

"Right! If I told anyone about what I see, they'd think I was crazy, and anyway, apart from you, I don't know anyone else who could see auras, even one as distinctive as Rickert's."

"Perhaps Doc Dabra knows of somebody."

"Yeah, but I've been looking for him and his shop for over a month... and nothing."

"Well, keep looking."

Since the hospital was within walking distance of home and my car was on the way to the wreckers... at least I wasn't in the trunk with a groove in my head from a tire iron... I decided to walk.

I wasn't very far along when it became clear my leg was hurting more than I expected when I set out. There was a sports bar along the way, and I limped in and ordered a beer. I guess it was a quiet sports night. The TV was tuned to a cable network on which was some kind of mystery show. There were only a few people in the bar. They were going about their personal business so no one but me was watching and I wasn't really following.

The program was produced in the city. Two commentators, a woman and a man, neither of whom could be over thirty, hosted it. They called themselves paranormal activity investigators. Their show, Paranormal Investigations, was about mysterious things they had discovered in and around town.

One place they talked about was a pretty average looking bungalow close to Amy Meecham's house. What had drawn them to it were reports that there was a pentagram and some odd symbols carved into the front door. Neighbors had told them it seemed to have been deserted for quite some time. The man who spent any time there only showed up off and on and was extremely unfriendly, they said. He would avoid them when he could and ignore them and their greetings when he couldn't.

The two commentators admitted they had snuck around the house, taking pictures through the windows. It turned out most of the rooms appeared empty except for one filled with books, bizarre occultist pictures and artifacts. Pentagrams and rune like drawings covered the wall they could see.

Something about the house with the pentagram on the door and a room full of bizarre occultist artifacts intrigued me, as did the two paranormal activity investigators. I was determined to find out more. At the end of the program, they gave the address of their website. I keyed it into my phone.

In had planned to go online to look up those paranormal activities investigators as soon as I got home. When I got there, I realized I was exhausted. The investigators would still be there tomorrow, unless, of course, they ran into Mr. Rickert. Told you I was tired. I asked Fitz to watch and let me know if any unwanted visitors, living or dead, showed up. "Sure thing, boss," he said, and I went off to bed.

33

Chap. 33. Paranormal Investigators

I woke from a deep sleep to discover every movement was uncomfortable, and for a few moments, I couldn't figure out why. Then, everything about the previous day came back to me. My leg hurt. There was a small, curved bruise on my forehead where I hit the steering wheel when my car jumped the curb. I remembered the man who was possessed by Rickert to drive his car into mine and when that failed, come at me with a tire iron. I remembered the flash of blue green light that came from my hands sending him back to his senses. I remembered Chivot, too, but most importantly, I remembered the paranormal investigators and the house they found with the pentagram on the door and the occult objects and symbols in the only finished room.

I also remembered I had planned to check their website to see if there was a way to get in touch with them. I really wanted to find out more about the house with the one room furnished with the occult objects and books.

First things first, I contacted my insurance company. A private eye without a car was a couch potato without a TV. Luckily, the car wasn't a write off, but it would take some time to repair. They offered me a loaner for the duration, so I was back on the job. Sadly, not the paying one. It meant I could get to the city for some house hunting if I could find out who those paranormal activity investigators were and could get in touch with them. So, I set out to do the number one job of most real life private investigators, research.

It didn't take long to drag up their website. There were a few videos on it, but not much information about who the investigators were or how to contact them. I found an email address on their site, but I guess they must be shy as it was the email of the cable network running the program. Short of searching out the base of operations for an obscure community cable network, this seemed to be my best chance of getting through to them.

I emailed the cable company. In it, I explained I was a detective investigating the case of a missing man with occult interests and would like to get in touch with the paranormal activity investigators about a story they aired on their show. I wanted to ask about the house with the room full of occult artifacts they had recently featured.

The reply was almost immediate. The investigators would be happy to meet with me. I should drop by the cable network site any day between 6pm and 10pm. If they were not there, they would likely be out on an investigation and someone in the office would let me know where to find them.

Admittedly, I didn't feel much like a wily sleuth from the world of fiction as I made my way through the inner city in search of the Columbus Community Cable, Offices and Studio. As it turns out, it was a place that anyone could easily miss. It was a smallish office building wedged between two large factories, one of which looked deserted, the other in what was apparently the truckload of gravel business. A dozen dump trucks loaded with gravel appeared to be coming and going in a constant swirl of dropping off gravel, picking more up and dropping it off again. Because of this, I nearly missed the CC Cable, Offices and Studios.

The red-haired receptionist, who couldn't have been more than eighteen, was focused on cleaning her fingernails as I entered. Her focus so intense, even with me standing right in front of her, she didn't notice until she reached for a bottle of nail polish on the curved desk. My presence clearly startled her. She pulled her hand back; her eyes were wide. "Oooh," she blurted, and then composing herself, "Sorry, I didn't see you come in. Can I help you?"

I told her I was looking for one of the paranormal activity investigators whose shows they aired on Friday evenings. "On Monday and Wednesday evenings too," she corrected, calling out, "Hey Vic, someone here to see you."

"Be right there," came a woman's voice from somewhere down the hall, "Have them take a seat."

"You heard her," said the red head, pointing to an array of chairs behind me, and then she seemed to lose interest, refocusing on the nail polish, which she opened and began meticulously applying to her fingernails.

Vic turned out to be an attractive blond woman in her late twenties carrying a mop. The new arrival had a pleasant-looking face, slightly less freckled than the red-haired younger version of her behind the desk. She was wearing baggy coveralls and carried a formidable looking mop in her hand. Smiling politely, she reached to her hand to me, realized she was holding the mop and set it to lean against the wall. "Victoria Ouldrud, with two u's," she smiled, "nice to meet you... ah..."

"Brendan Bannon, with two n's," I chuckled as I took her hand to shake it.

"Well, Mr. Bannon, what can I do for you?"

"I emailed you the other day. I'm a private investigator, myself. I'm working on behalf of a client who's gone missing. Apparently, he was very interested in the occult. I was interested in the house you found with the odd artifacts and markings you had investigated on last Friday's show. I believe it might hold some clue to his disappearance."

It wasn't exactly the truth, but it wasn't exactly a lie, either. Her expression was vague for a moment, and then she smiled and raised a finger. "Yes, I remember the place. It was quite mysterious. We would have spent more time investigating it, but we weren't actually invited, if you get my meaning."

"I do, but I would very much like to take a look at it. Could you direct me there?"

"I can do better than that. If you wait awhile for Don to get here, we can all go."

She turned to leave, reaching for the mop leaning against the wall, then stopped, looked back at me and giggled. "Oh, this is so exciting. I have to change and prepare the cameras," and she disappeared back into the corridor; the forgotten mop stood there leaning against the wall.

Red the Receptionist had gone back to painting her nails. The magazines on the coffee table by the chairs were several ancient ones about media business. Most were old fashion magazines. There were a couple of paperback picture books. One was titled The Supernatural, the other was Paranormal Universe, both of which I had spent hours pondering over when I first realized I could see dead people. Nothing to read, so I watched Red as she methodically applied nail polish to one finger after another. It was about as exciting as watching paint dry, which, in a sense, it was.

Eventually the doors opened and in stepped a bearded man in his late twenties wearing jeans and a leather jacket, carrying a camera bag over his shoulder. Red was so disinterested I thought I was seeing another ghost. That was until he leaned over the desk towards Red and said, "Hey Kath, where's Vicky?"

Without looking up from her nail painting, she said, "Down the hall doing something. Getting a camera, I think."

He made no response, but turned to me, "you the private eye?"

I nodded. He stepped over to me, hand outstretched. "Donny, Donny Brassard, paranormal activity investigator,"

Shaking his hand, I introduced myself.

"So, you've watched the show," he said. "What do you think of it?"

Before I could answer, Vicky stepped into the room. She was wearing jeans and a leather jacket similar to Donny's. A strap over her shoulder held a large case. "Camera," she grinned, tapping the case.

"State of the art," boasted Donny who then added, "So, you want to see the weird place from yesterday's show."

I told him I did, and he said, "Let's go then. You can join us in the van or follow in your car."

When I told him I'd follow in my car, he seemed relieved. He reached over to Vicky and put his hand on her shoulder, guiding her to the door. He did, however, if you'll pardon the expression, leave her holding the bag.

34

Chap. 34. Rickert's Arsonist

The drive to the house took about twenty minutes. The van with the large

PAI.com logo a cartoon ghost picture on the back doors assured that. We were able to proceed at a good pace and no cars came out of driveways or side streets to T-Bone me, so that was a bonus.

We turned off onto a tree lined side street. The houses were set back from the road. They looked like good, solid middle-class homes, not huge, but tasteful and well cared for, as were their front gardens. The van stopped in front of an unremarkable looking house with no front garden and Donny pointed through the window at it, then indicated he was going to go farther up the street to park. I followed and parked behind him. The sun was setting as we walked back towards the house, casting long shadows of the trees over the road.

Several ragged looking conical cedars lined the driveway, and we stayed close to them as we made our way to the door. The last rays of sunlight reflected off it, revealing the pentagram and indecipherable runes scratched on it. I was grateful for the neighbors' conveniently high hedge as we along the side of the house towards the window into the room with the artifacts. There was enough light to reveal what looked like ancient fertility statuary, some mounted animal skulls and a bookshelf crammed with old and well-used books. Vicky took the camera out of the case and was adjusting the lenses. I had pulled myself up as high as I could to get a better view of what was inside. Vicky held the camera on her shoulder, so it was high enough to get a reasonable interior shot.

I spent some time studying the objects and wishing I could get closer. As it grew darker, some artifacts gave off a faint green glow. That wasn't good. As I was noticing the glow, there was a cacophony of sirens off in the distance. Looking to past the houses on the other side of the street, I could see a flickering light against the darkening sky. It may have been several streets away, but close enough for the sounds to carry clearly.

Moments later, a car pulled up and stopped in front of the house. Having not been "invited", we moved back to hide behind the cedars lining the drive. The car door opened, and a large, heavyset man stepped out, carrying what appeared to be a gas can. He sported a red aura with black fringes. "My lord," squeaked Vicky, "what the hell is that? I've never seen anything like it. Do you see it, Donny?"

"Yes," his voice wavering ever so slightly, "I've never seen that color of red before, and... the black tips."

I got a lot of information from those few words. The paranormal activity investigators could see auras. What's more, I knew that aura. He moved easily up the driveway to the door and was reaching over the lintel, looking for a key. This was definitely Rickert's place. He was here and from the gas can in his puppet's hand, up to no good. Whatever he was up to, I wasn't going to leave him to it. I raised my hands palms out towards him. A greenish blue stream of light came from them, striking Rickert's possessed servant. There was a screech, and the red and black aura was extinguished.

"Was that lightning?" asked a shaken Vicky of no-one in particular.

"I don't know," answered Donny, "but the aura is gone."

The man at the door looked quickly around. I had stepped out past the trees for a clear shot, and that's where I was when he saw me. He let out a roar and ran straight for me. I expected him to be confused, wondering where he was, not to be charging at me like an angry bull. "You bastard," he shouted, "what did you do to me? You stole my power," and he was on me.

He got three or four good punches in until Donny rushed in to pull him off me. I could barely see the formerly possessed man through the stars that filled my vision. It was enough to show an intense anger. He must have seen Vicky with the camera. He shouted again and raced back to his car. Seconds later, tires squealing, he executed a U-turn, nearly flipping the car and was off down the street. Vicky was in my face asking me if I was alright.

I have to say, the residents of this area did an especially good job of minding their own business. Nobody came out a door and as far as I could see, which at the moment wasn't very, nobody was looking out a window either. Acting as if I belonged, I walked up to the door. The gas tank Rickert's man was carrying stank of gas. I wondered if he was the reason, we still heard those not so distant sirens. I reached above the door and found the key. "Don't worry," I lied, as I unlocked the door. "I have his wife's permission to go inside. He's likely dead, so the place is hers, anyway."

"Do you think he died in there?" Asked Vicky.

"That I can guarantee, however, who knows what equally disconcerting things we might find."

"I'm sorry," said a mystified Donny, "Why are we doing this. Shouldn't we be calling the cops?"

"Wait, wait," stuttered Vicky, "what did you do to that guy? You saw the red and black aura, didn't you? You put your hands up and that hideous aura disappeared. What are you?"

"Private investigator on a case," was my only reply, and I walked down the hall to the room with the occult artifacts and the books.

"Phew, this place stinks," said Donny, bashing his open hand in front of his face to fan some odor away.

He was right, it stank. Stale blood, burnt animal hair, decomposing rodents in small cages around the floor. Ignoring it all, I walked over to the books. Most were filed neatly in the bookcase. A few were scattered on a small table, which they shared with an assortment of scratches and burns. A quick scan informed me one of the more ancient books was the Necromancium.

There was an envelope being used as a bookmark in it. I wanted nothing to do with looking into it, but I pulled out the envelope. Confirmation: the envelope was addressed to one Jerry Rickert. "Okay," I said, "I've got what I wanted. We can leave now."

"What do you mean, leave, this is exciting; a treasure-trove for or program," the camera in her hands, Vicky kept on shooting as she spoke.

"I have a horrible feeling a lot of this stuff could be dangerous and," I added, "I'm not sure, but I think we tripped an alarm when we came into the room."

I wasn't sure if there even was an alarm, but I had a powerful feeling we needed to get out of there. Reluctantly, the two paranormal investigators joined me as I headed for the door. As I passed through the door, there was an enormous inhalation of air from the living room.

It was as if someone had turned on an enormous vacuum cleaner. Rickert must have rigged some sort of protection. The pull would have knocked Vicky over if I hadn't grabbed her arm and drew her through the door. We were barely outside when the door slammed shut, grazing Donny's right shoulder as he struggled to keep Vicky on her feet. You think someone had shot him; his yell of pain was so loud.

"Let's get out of here," shouted Donny, rubbing his shoulder as he ran down the driveway and up the street to the van.

"Wait there," he called, "I'll bring the van around and pick you up."

By the time he started the van, Vicky and I were at my car. I climbed in, but before I could get the key in the slot, Vicky was knocking on the passenger. She pulled the door open, dropped the camera on the floor, and climbed into the passenger seat. She rolled down the window as Donny pulled up with the van and yelled, "I'm going with him. See you back at the office."

He pulled away as I got my car running. I made a u turn on the street, carefully avoiding the neatly trimmed hedge across the street. Through the corner of my eye, I could see Vicky giving me a long look. "Who the hell are you, mister? I think you have some serious explaining to do."

For a split second, her no nonsense tone sent me back to grade six and my teacher from hell, Mrs. Jenkins, not my best memory.

35

Chap. 35. Spirit Zappers

On the drive back to Columbus Community Cable offices, Vicky grilled me like a TV cop. "What did you know about that house before we went? Who was that guy with the red and black aura? You can see auras, can't you? What did you do to him? What was he talking about, 'Take his power?' How did you know to get out of there when we did?"

Some of her questions I could answer straight up. I told her I could see auras, and I suspected the guy with the aura had come to destroy the house. The red and black aura apparently belonged to someone contaminated by evil. As to what I had done to him, I told her I pissed him off and by 'losing his power' he must have meant his focus.

I knew she wasn't buying it. She wanted to know what I had done to piss him off because all she had seen was me stepping out and turning the palms of my hand towards him. "You couldn't have thrown anything at him with your hands like that."

Damn, she was too observant. She might have been shooting movies in the place, but she was watching me carefully, too.

She was a good interrogator because she was well on the way to wearing me down, when my phone rang.

The loaner I was driving didn't have a Bluetooth, so I pulled my phone from my pocket and handed it to her. "Could you answer that for me, please?"

She said, "Hello," after which there was a pause, then she added, "Victoria Ouldrud, Paranormal Activities Investigator... Yes, he's right here... car has no Bluetooth. I'll put you on speaker. One second."

"Someone named Jenny, wants to speak with you," and she held the phone up near my right ear.

"Hi, Jenny."

"What's going on, Brendan? Why is there someone in the car with you, I think she said, paranormal investigator? You alright?"

"It's a long story Jenny, I'll get back to you on that. So, what's up?"

"I wanted to let you know fire destroyed Amy Meecham's home earlier this evening and there was another attack on Fred. Hospital staff were able to stop the assailant before he had a chance to hurt him."

"And Amy, how is she?"

"She's fine. She wasn't home. Anyway, I've got to go. Call me in the morning."

I was going to tell her about the possessed man with the gas can. He was probably the same person who set Amy Meecham's place on fire. I wasn't quite ready to reveal all I knew to Vicky and Donny, so I chose not to say any more. Instead, I told her I would call her in the morning and said goodbye.

When Jenny was offline, Vicky shut my phone off and gave it back to me. "Who are Amy and Fred Meecham and why did your

Jenny feel she needed to call you and tell you about the attack on Fred and the fire at Amy's house?"

I was going to make up a story, then thought, "what the hell," so I told her a little about Amy and Fred, touching on Rickert, but I was not quite ready to tell her Rickert was a powerful and dangerous living spirit. "And he's the guy who owned the house we were in? Was that the person whose power you took away? I know you will not tell me what the power was, but I'll ask, anyway. Was that guy Rickert, or did he work for him? Do you think he burned down Amy's house?"

"You could say he was working for Rickert, and it is likely he was also the arsonist who had set the fire at Amy Meecham's house."

We arrived at the cable building, and I stopped to let her out. She hesitated before she left, handing me a business card, and asked if I had one to exchange. Luckily, I had some business cards for Brendan Bannon PI printed up and had a few with me. I took one only slightly bent from Rickert's man's attack from my shirt pocket and gave it to her.

"We'll be meeting again soon," she stated rather firmly; it didn't sound like she was talking about a social get together.

I wanted to meet with them again. They could see auras, so they were especially interesting to me, but first I needed to consult with Jenny. By the time I got home, it was definitely too late to call her. It could wait for tomorrow.

"Well, that was quite the adventure," came a voice from somewhere nearby.

Not so long ago, a voice coming out of nowhere in an apartment I should have been alone in, would have had me running for the door. Now, it barely startled me. I knew instantly it was Fitz, my often invisible, but ever present, companion.

"Don't worry, boss, I'm on the lookout. No one is getting in here tonight, living or dead, without me knowing it. And, if I know it, you know it, so you can grab the baseball bat you have by your bed or hold up your spirit zappers, so get some sleep."

So now my hands were spirit zappers. Well, I guess they were, so between them and the bat, along with Fitz on watch, I was safe enough to sleep soundly, Which I must have because before I knew it, sunlight was streaming through my bedroom window.

A short time later, the day was underway. I called Jenny and told her the whole story, the paranormal activities investigation cable show, the cable offices and paranormal investigators, Vicky and Donny. I told her about the house and the items inside, as well as the envelope confirming it belonged to Rickert. Something I was certain of the moment I saw the red and black aura around the potential arsonist. It delighted me when Jenny, instead of accusing me of a B and E, laughed and said, "There's the advantage of being a PI, Brendan, you don't need to track down a judge for a warrant."

I suspected she understood what we were doing was outside the range of standard police procedure. There were things Doc Dabra said to make me think there was something more serious going on here than the occasional obsessively evil ghost.

Jenny told me she was off work for a few days and would like to meet those paranormal activities investigators. It intrigued her they, too, could see auras. It might just work out for everyone involved. I wanted to find out more about them, too, and I couldn't forget Vicky's words as she closed the car door.

I called the cable network and I assume it was Red, or whatever her name was, who answered, "Columbus Community Cable, how can I help you?"

It sounded to me as if the last thing she ever wanted to do was help any caller. If there was a way of sounding totally bored, she was the poster girl for it. I asked for Vicky, telling her it was PI Bannon. "Hold on," she drawled, "I'll get her."

She didn't even bother to cover the speaker as she shouted a frustrated, "Hey Vicky, there's a phone call for you. It's that PI guy who was here last night."

I heard her set the phone down on the desk and go back to whatever important task I had taken her from. Oh, to be a teenager.

When Vicky finally made it to the phone, I told her that my investigations partner and I wished to meet with her. We just needed somewhere private. She couldn't have sounded more different on the phone than Red, or whoever it was, who first answered. It wasn't a problem; she said. There was no one around the building until the afternoon, and there was a nice conference room on the upper floor no one ever used. We could meet there. Tomorrow, eleven would be fine. She'd let Donny know so he could take time off work to join us.

36

Chap. 36. Meet Fitz

I arrived in front of The Columbus Cable building just before eleven. Jenny was already there. It was a sunny spring day and Jenny was waiting for me, leaning against the hood of her car. She was wearing track pants and a light jacket thrown over a graphic T-shirt. I think it said "Gandolph Rules," above a dark face with a long flowing beard and wearing a large pointy hat. Amazing! I'd known her all this time, never suspecting she was a Lord of the Rings fan.

She greeted me with, "Seen any sign of Rickert?"

"Not since the day before yesterday. And, how are you?"

"Pretty good. I have a week off from work. I guess I'll just loaf around and look for evil spirits. You?"

"Oh, you know, privately investigating things. Shall we go in?"

Sure enough, Red, or Kath, or whatever her name was at the reception desk, looking as bored as she had sounded when I called yesterday. She was industriously texting on her phone, only looking up when she sent it. I heard the whoosh. "Vicky!"

She called.

Moments later, Vicky stepped into the room. She wore distressed jeans... you pay extra for the holes... white sneakers and a Stanford University sweatshirt. "You went to Stanford," I gasped.

"Oh," she looked down at the logo on her shirt, "no, just locally. Picked this up on a trip west last year. I like the feel."

She looked up and saw Jenny. "Hi," she said as Donny peaked his head into the room

"I'm sorry," I apologized as Jenny said "hi," back. "This is my investigations partner Jenny."

I'm not sure why I did, but I added, "Detective Sergeant Jennifer Wenstead, Metro police."

Their eyes went wide. Donny pulled back into the hall and nearly out of sight. "Just call me, Jenny," Jenny said.

She always knew how to deal with pressure situations. Vicky immediately relaxed, but Donny continued to look a little wary. Jenny gave him a great big smile. "You know it is legal here, now."

Donny didn't know where to look. "Relax," she added, "I'm on holidays. Shall we head to the conference room."

Those were like magic words. Donny visibly relaxed. "It's this way," he said, leading us to an elevator.

The conference room was spacious, with an enormous oval table designed to seat about twenty people. The chairs were solid and comfortably cushioned. The room itself was wood paneled except for the outer wall that comprised wainscot beneath large windows stretching the width of the wall and reaching from about three feet high all the way to the ceiling. The view of the factory where those many dump trucks were loading and unloading gravel was spectacular. Unfortunately, there were no curtains. The four of us took seats at one end of the table.

Having introduced Jenny, I felt we needed introductions all around, so I held my hand out towards Vicky, and looked at Jenny. "Jenny, this is Vicky…"

I paused to let her add her last name. "Ouldrud, with two u's," she said, executing a polite half bow.

I turned to Donny, "And Donny…"

"Brassard," he completed.

Jenny nodded at each of them, then turned to me, looking for an explanation.

"Vicky and Donny are… what was it you called yourself?" I directed my question to Donny.

"Paranormal activities investigators. PIA.com and on YouTube," he responded proudly.

"So, Vicky, Donny," Jenny's tone was police officer serious, "tell me what you saw the other night when you were with Brendan."

"To begin with," said Vicky, raising her hand to halt Donny from speaking, "we were moving around the house looking through the windows. Donny and I have been there before. We took a video of the front door and a few minutes more through the side window of the living room. It was pretty hard to see, so then we went to speak with some neighbors."

"When we were there with Mr. Bannon, we had been looking through the windows. I was shooting a video. That's when I noticed that as it grew dark, some things in the room took on a slightly greenish glow. We heard the car pull up in front and slipped behind the bushes. We saw a man step out of his car carrying some kind of container. What really stood out about him was a red and black aura. Both Donny and I see auras. It's part of the reason we started our paranormal activities website and YouTube channel. We've seen a lot of auras, but we've never seen anything like that before."

She turned to Donny, who shook his head. "Never," he said.

Vicky continued, "The man with the weird aura was at the front door when Mr. Bannon stepped out from the bushes and held up his hands to point at him. Immediately, the red and black aura disappeared and a dirty blue one replaced it. The man then yelled and attacked Mr. Bannon saying he had taken away his power."

I felt the description of what had happened was about right, although I didn't remember the dirty blue aura replacing Rickert's black and red one. Jenny was about to ask another question when, from the corner of my eye, I saw Fitz appear very close to Vicky. He began waving and smiled in my direction when Vicky seemed to go berserk. "What is that? What's there? Help me, please, there is something beside me. Help."

Fitz vanished as quickly as he had arrived. Jenny gave me a questioning look. "Fitz," I said, "he materialized. for me, anyway, right beside Vicky."

"One way of answering the question I was about to ask." said Jenny.

Meanwhile, Vicky had jumped up and was standing near the door. Her eyes were wide in terror, and her voice was shaking. "What was that? What happened there?"

There was no doubt Vicky was on the verge of panic, so I got up and stepped over to her. I placed a hand on her shoulder, and she calmed. "You just had an encounter with a genuine living spirit," I said, "his name is Fitz. Nothing to be afraid of."

"You mean ghost? There was a ghost here... like a dead person?"

"Sorry," I said, "I guess we all figured paranormal investigator and all, you would have some familiarity with the spirit world."

"It was a ghost? Right there beside me?" She was still shaking.

"Actually, very few people can sense the presence of a living spirit. Fitz would not intend to scare you. He is, in fact, quite a decent... not person... spirit."

That didn't really sound right to me, but I let it drop. Jenny spoke up. "You have a very rare gift and I'll tell you from personal experience, it takes some getting used to. Oh, and you should be able to hear them speak as well."

"Do you want me to call him back," I asked.

"Is it safe?" Vicky's voice came out, barely above a squeak.

"Perfectly," said Jenny.

"Ok, call him back."

I called Fitz and the gentleman he was, he appeared at the far end of the room. "Say hello to Vicky, Fitz," I said.

What to Jenny and to Vicky was sound from out of nowhere, Fitz spoke. "I'm so sorry to have frightened you, mistress Vicky, and I am delighted to make your acquaintance."

Although I've done my best to avoid profanity in the need for clarity, I will quote miss Vicky verbatim: "Holy shit, they're real! Sorry, oh shit, yeah, nice, I think, to meet you, Mr. Fitz."

The entire time, Donny sat frozen in place, his wide, terrified eyes glancing from Vicky to the back of the room where Fitz was and back again as if he was watching a tennis match. Watching him and trying desperately not to laugh, I said to Fitz, "Fitz, this is Donny."

"Hi Donny," Fitz said, but Donny continued to sit there as if in a trance, saying nothing and watching that invisible tennis match.

37

Chap. 37. A Weird Aura

Fitz's appearance in the cable company's conference room had created quite a stir, and that was understating it. The discovery of a talent neither knew they had freaked out both Vicky and Donny. Jenny and I decided we should all get out of there for the moment. A short time later, in a dark corner of a nearby bar, Jenny and I sipping our coffees while Vicky and Donny had ordered something stronger. We were able to calm them enough so that they opened up.

Donny admitted to only half believing in ghosts and hauntings when he suggested to fellow university freshman Victoria Ouldrud, who seemed keen on things paranormal. They start a website looking for and reviewing the haunted houses in and around the city. They had been doing it for nearly eight years. In that time, they have gone from a simple website to YouTube, a successful blog, and for the last two years, a video program on community cable station. Even a few cable networks around the country had picked up the show.

Vicky was more of a believer, but Donny had to admit that

despite all the success, small time as it was, he was still honestly skeptical. Then, about four years ago they came across an optometrist's store and office that seemed to magically show up in a mall they had passed by every day. The back door was open, and they went in. They found nothing there but a few chairs and a device that looked like binoculars. They took turns at the binoculars but saw nothing. It seems shortly after that they began to see auras around people.

They apparently didn't make the connection, but I did. They just thought it was a good story and so, at least between them, they decided their interesting vision had begun in there. It was simply an optometrist's office. They really did not know why they had gained the power. So, I told them. It surprised them they had got it right. Then I did a full Doc Dabra and told them they always had the ability and looking into the binocular like device only focused it.

They hadn't realized that they could sense living spirits and hear them, too. They probably never got as close to a living spirit before Fitz and since these spirits are generally quiet, never heard them. That would change. "What do you mean by that," asked Vicky.

"If you spend any time around me or Jenny, you are going to encounter lots of living spirits,"

"Why do you call them living spirits, aren't they ghosts?"

It may have been an awkwardly stated question, but one that needed an answer. "Ghosts," I told her, "are manifestations of the dead that may, or may not exist. Living spirits are spirits of people who have died that continue on after death. These living spirits can stay close to this plain of existence or move on to somewhere else. I don't really understand how that works. I was told that sometimes the spirits are bound to earth because of the displacement of a body part. I'm not sure if that's exactly true," and I turned to look at Fitz who was standing behind Jenny.

Fitz smiled and shrugged, and I continued, "Living spirits are basically the same in death as they were in life. A gentle person will be a gentler spirit, an angry person an angry spirit, and a caring person, a caring spirit. The only changes I've seen regarding these spirits are when, while they were alive, they fostered evil. After death, this evil not only lingers, but in some cases can grow."

Jenny took over, proving she paid attention and did her homework. "Evil spirits can learn to possess humans and manipulate them for their own purposes. When that happens, the aura of the one possessed takes on a bizarre coloration."

"So," said Vicky, controlling her voice to hide her fear, "the man with the red and black aura was being possessed? Why did he get so angry with Brendan when he canceled the possession?"

"Good question," was all Jenny said, turning to face me.

We all wanted answers, and the best I could do was speculate. "I believe our villain, a certain evil spirit we know by the name of Jerry Rickert, is perfecting his possession ability. Previously, he only possessed the mentally frail. Then it seemed as if he could possess anyone if he got to them while they were distracted or not paying attention. In the person's case at the house, I believe he and Jerry had somehow struck a deal to work together."

"Just think of what a person with a criminal bent could accomplish with the help of a living spirit."

There was silence around our table while we all let that worrisome bit of news settle in. The silence was broken by Vicky asking, "So what does this have to do with Donny and I?"

It had everything to do with them, although just yet I wasn't prepared to say. When they were around, there were two more sets of eyes watching for Jerry and one of his possessed. As well as that, they were to some extent known in the city and surrounding area from their cable program. If something mysterious was going on, one of their viewers would likely let them know. With dangerous people, living or dead, on the loose, so to speak, it wouldn't hurt to have some reliable informants. What I did say was, "With your extensive knowledge of the city and the information you gather from your viewers and from your research, you could help us track down and deal with any strange and ghostly behavior. You know, by investigating paranormal activities."

I could see it intrigued Vicky. Donny looked a touch skeptical, so I added, "and we could let you know about interesting locations and events you could use for your show."

It was clear this resonated with Donny. He looked up and smiled. His eyes turned skyward, and his head tilted to the right as he considered the possibilities. Score one for the Brendan.

We made the deal and now had two more partners; two more believers to watch for red and black auras; two more supporters to call on when tracking down the unconventional burial locations of the missing dead. We exchanged cell numbers and email addresses. I signaled for Fitz to come closer. As he neared Vicky, she flinched, then looked at me asking, "Fitz?"

I nodded, and she immediately relaxed. It was a positive sign we had made a breakthrough in more ways than one with our paranormal activities investigators. Donny was oblivious to Fitz's presence, but I suspected this was a typical state for him.

38

Chap. 38. Team Building

The ebb and flow of life seemed to be more flow than ebb, but for a few days things were quiet. Rickert had not once tried to kill me. Although a good sign, it didn't make me feel much better. I knew the longer he avoided me, the sooner he would return and the harder he would strike. His capabilities were mounting, making him more of a danger to me and society in general.

Doc Dabra was nowhere to be found, leaving me to depend on the limited abilities of Jenny and the paranormal investigators and my two bare hands. Yeah, I had the sight, but it was so strong; it was hard to discern whether someone I was seeing was a living person or a living spirit. There were clues; living persons had auras, living spirits didn't unless they were particularly evil and were possessing someone.

At the moment, I only knew of one living spirit who could do that, and the vivid aura the person he possessed projected was a dead giveaway, no pun intended. Even so, in an anxious moment, I might be too concerned with my personal safety to be looking around for the presence or absence of often faint auras. To that end, I was cautious, avoiding large crowds and confining myself to my home, car, or a coffee shop with Jenny.

I could never take my guard down, so it was almost a relief when Vicky called to tell me they had received a call from a viewer about something strange in a park near her house. It was a sunny warm day and on days like this there were usually lots of people relaxing, playing or walking around, enjoying the park. Only a die-hard PAI watcher would notice that even the park regulars were turning away at the entrances. A small group of people, unfamiliar to the viewer, we're standing around on the park grounds.

Vicky and Donny followed up and called back to report what the viewer was observing was indeed the case. People heading for the park reached the entrances and immediately turned away, while a group of nondescript people with faded auras seemed to be aimlessly circling the park grounds. When the two investigators approached the park entrance, they found they really didn't want to enter. They fought the feeling, saying it was like pushing through gel to do so. Once inside the park, they confronted several of the people milling about. The ones they approached all said the same thing "tell Bannon he's waiting," and that was all.

When I heard that, a chill ran down my spine. That park was the last place I wanted to go. But I knew I had to. I called Jenny and told her I was on my way to the city and the name of the park I was heading to. She said she knew it and would meet me at a nearby parking lot, adding for me to be careful. No problem there.

For her, the drive was a short one. For me, not so much. By the time I had followed all the GPS instructions and arrived next to the park, could see Vicky and Donny seated on a bench and Jenny in her working attire, a conservative woman's suit waiting by the gate. She waved when she saw me and pointed over her shoulder to indicate the parking area. I pulled in, found a spot, and parked.

A few moments later, I joined Jenny at the park entrance. It was a large city park enclosed by low hedges with a grassed area that was large and open. A small, well tended copse of trees marked the far end. The cultivated informality implied a popular recreational site, but as Vicky had informed us, today, it was nearly empty except for the small number of aimless wanderers and the two paranormal activities investigators seated on a bench close by.

Together, Jenny and I entered the park. Jenny seemed to put some effort into getting through the gate. I felt nothing unusual. Was that because of what Doc Dabra termed my increasing abilities, or was it because the powerful living spirit of Jerry Rickert had left it open for me? Perhaps it was a bit of both.

Jenny and I had joined Vicky and Donny at the park bench when a large man stepped from behind the trees at the far end of the park. As he came toward us, his red and black aura was plain to see. It wavered around him, sending flame-like black wisps into the air. The others no longer aimlessly lined up on either side of him. I didn't like the look of it. Nothing good was going to happen. I needed to stop it. I raised my palms in their direction, and a blue green stroke of lightning hit the man with the red and black aura. Immediately, the aura disappeared. Unlike the previous times, I hadn't driven Rickert off. Instead, his living spirit wearing a filigreed robe of red and black was there in front.

I held my palms out toward him, and he held his out toward me. It is hard to describe what happened next. The blue green lightning played across Rickert and those standing with him.

They all seemed to be immobile. Also sensed waves of energy coming from Rickert, holding me and my cohorts who had stood to stand beside me equally immobile.

To anyone seeing us in the park, we probably would look like we were forming some kind of tableau, representing some incomprehensible standoff. Four unmoving people, one with hands raised and palms held outward, facing off across a space separating them from eight other people equally unmoving. They would likely wonder if these were actual people, as the tableau persisted well past the time when the participants should show significant discomfort.

As I stood there, the waves of energy from Rickert made my head swim. As each wave pressed into me, my vision dimmed, as did the blue green energy from my hands. I was getting the worst of the battle, for that's what it was, a battle that would reveal who was more powerful and destroy the one who wasn't, and I was seriously losing. There was a pounding pain in my head. My arms ached. I was desperate to drop them, but I knew I couldn't. I could barely stand but was able to call out, "help."

I felt a tentative touch on my right shoulder as Jenny struggled to put her hand there. A surge of power flowed through me, my vision cleared, and the energy from my hands grew brighter. On my left side, Vicky must have sensed this, because she slowly forced her hand against my shoulder. The energy from my hands grew stronger, as did my resolve. A third burst of energy told me that somehow, I was drawing from Donny as well.

As the lightning from my hands increased, I felt Rickert's energy waver. I slowly drew my hands together to focus on him and the waves of lightning blended together, striking him chest high and washing in licks of flame across his body. I could see it startled him. He hadn't expected the resistance that I

169

was offering, and I was slowly overpowering him. The energy flowing from him weakened. I pressed my eyes tight shut and, in my mind, tried to send more lightening at Rickert. I felt a burst of energy from my hands, and an immense wave of exhaustion passed over me.

Opening my eyes, I saw Rickert, his eyes wide in disbelief as the last vestiges of blue green energy coursed over him and as I watched in disbelief, he began to shrink, growing smaller and smaller as the blue green energy engulfed him. Still hanging waist high in the air, a micro-sized Rickert let out a loud, size defying scream, rolled into a diminishing ball, and vanished. Everything went dark, and I collapsed to the ground, feeling absolutely empty.

Next thing I knew, I was slumped on a park bench with Jenny and Vicky looking down at me, worried expressions on both their faces. I sat up and looked around. Rickert and has henchmen were truly gone. Several locals were already in the park setting up picnic blankets, walking arm in arm, throwing frisbees. "How long was I out," I asked Jenny.

Scanning the already growing numbers of visitors to the park, she smiled. "Oh, about fifteen minutes. The moment you dropped your arms and there was that strange scream, the others, I guess the regulars, began arriving."

"What happened?" Vicky wanted to know.

Donny leaned over her shoulder. "Yeah," he said, "I don't know what happened except I have to admit, it scared me crapless."

No question. Those were the most words Donny had strung together at one time since we first met.

I told them about Rickert appearing after I threw him out of the one he was possessing and the waves of energy coming from him. "We felt those," said Jenny. "We couldn't move while it was happening."

"I know," I said. "The same thing was happening to Rickert's men. But you could move enough when I called for help. I don't know if you realized it, but when you put your hands on my shoulders, I drew energy from you. It was the only reason I could stop him."

"I knew something was happening. The moment I touched your shoulder, my hand tingled," said Vicky.

"Mine, too," added Jenny.

"I touched Vicky's shoulder and felt the same," said Donny.

"Nice," I grinned, "teamwork. I guess we're a team now."

Then Vicky went and spoiled the moment. "Is this Rickert spirit gone forever, or will he come back?"

All I could offer was hope. As far as her question, everyone's question, I had no definitive answer.

39

Chap. 39. Fly in the Ointment

Leaving the park, we all made our way to a nearby restaurant. We were exhausted and drained, and curiously hungry. I sensed we all shared the same hopefulness that we had experienced the last of the living spirit of Jerry Rickert. For most of the time, we sat in silence. None of us had much to say. We ate quickly. Each of us wanted nothing more than to get home and get some sleep.

They lived nearby, but I would spend an hour or more on the highway, so I begged my leave and headed for my car. Jenny joined me. "You're not convinced, are you?"

"Don't know. I saw him shrink into a tiny ball and vanish. I think it was the end of him, but I really don't know enough about the power of the necromancers or the abilities of Rickert. He's a ghost, damn it. He shouldn't even be here. He's dead, he should be gone." I did a quick look around to see if Fitz had heard me.

Luckily, he was nowhere to be seen. If he heard me, I would apologize to him later. "I wish Doc Dabra would show up. He'd have the answers."

"No sign of him?" Asked Jenny.

"Not for months."

A few minutes later, I was in the car heading for the highway home. I turned up the radio and rolled down the windows as I went. I didn't want to fall asleep behind the wheel.

Traffic was light, and the loaner was smooth and effortless to drive. I was lost in my thoughts, the radio blaring, the wind whistling around me, when an exasperated voice broke through my reverie. "Could you turn down that hideous racket, please?"

I didn't notice it at first until it was repeated, "Really Brendan, could you please shut off that horrible noise."

I glanced toward the sound of the voice and to my horror there was self-proclaimed Brother Chivot. "The radio, Brendan; could you turn it off? It is very annoying."

Reaching over, I shut the radio off, resisting the impulse to look at Chivot. I asked in an unnecessarily loud voice, "What the hell are you doing here."

"Really Brendan, profanity. I just came to thank you for leading me to Jerry Rickert."

"But he's dead... I mean, I've driven him off to, I don't know, eternity."

"Sorry to dissuade you of your self-congratulatory delusion, but you have not sent Brother Rickert to any distant eternity. His eternity is right here and after he regenerates, he and I shall combine to bring righteous justice to this world."

In a blend of sheer terror and absolute rage, I hollered, "Why can't you just leave me alone."

"Sorry, Brendan, my boy, no can do. You see, you are the fly in our ointment, the roadblock to the furtherance of our plans. We have to remove you. As long as you're around, I regret to say, because I've grown fond of you, you are a problem. Oh yes, as are your associates. And, we will not be foiled."

With those words, Chivot vanished.

For the rest of the drive home, I was wide awake. I forced myself to focus on the road, as I tuned in an easy listening station on the radio. I needed something to soothe my seething thoughts. Arriving home, the very first thing I did was pour myself a strong drink, opening a bottle of single malt scotch someone had bought me for Christmas a few years back. I took a long sip, then dialed Jenny's number.

"Brendan," Jenny yawned. "What's the problem?"

Even half asleep, Jenny knew me well enough to realize whenever I called, I was going to present her with a problem. "Sorry to wake you, but I have some bad news."

"Ok, let me have it. What's the bad news," she groaned.

"Rickert isn't gone."

"And you know that, how?"

"Chivot dropped into my car on the way home to tell me."

Her voice, dripping with irony, Jenny said, "Well, that was real nice of him"

"Yeah. You got it... not so much. He told me when Rickert's back online, or whatever... he said regenerated... they were going to join up, and...."

I paused long enough for her to snap, "And what?"

"I'm to be their prime target. Apparently, I am the fly in their ointment, and I need to be removed. As if that wasn't bad enough, you and our newfound friends, the TV investigators are next."

Now she was interested. "Why would he tell you that?"

"Said he owed me one for introducing, maybe a poor choice of words there, bringing him in contact with Rickert."

"Oh, lovely."

More sarcasm. I suppose having your life threatened by a ghost will bring that out.

I sensed a bit more control in Jenny's voice as she asked, "O.K., so how long will hit be for Rickert to get back, in your words, online?"

"Good question," and as usual for Jenny, it was always right to the point, "I do have to say, he didn't look so good when he was being compressed into a tinier and timer whirling ball before vanishing; several days, I'd think."

"But you don't know for sure."

"I know little of anything, Jenny, but I'm pretty darn sure we have a few days."

I'm not sure why, but I was certain we had more than a few days. What I had done to Rickert was something he was going to take some time to come back from. It was only a feeling, but a strong one. Call it my spidey sense, but I was convinced it would be a good while before he and Chivot would be ready to come for me. I was, however, quite certain I could not share this conviction with the others. For them, only time would tell.

Jenny yawned. "I'm exhausted, Brendan, and I have to get up for work tomorrow. I hope you're right about Rickert. Let's just say I trust you enough to wish you a good evening. As for me, I'm going back to sleep. We'll talk again in a day or two if Rickert hasn't made his comeback before then. Night!"

Jenny may go back to sleep, but I was still too energized from earlier. Tired, yes. Exhausted, for sure. Sleepy, not a chance! I sat back on my beloved old reclining chair and lifted the bottle of whisky to my lips. A flood of flame shot down my throat as I took a swig. It reminded me why I didn't drink much. I went to the fridge to find something a little less extreme.

Stretching back into the comforting confines of my recliner, I reviewed the events of the day. In the park, battling Rickert, I had sensed a deep terror of the forces lined up against me, yet at the same time, there was exhilaration as the energy flowed through my body. I had never felt so powerful. For a moment I wanted to wave my fists and shout, "Bring it on Rickert; Bring it on Chivot." Then it struck me. What was I thinking? These were spirits of the dead. They were both evil and horrendously powerful. I was a small town guy who aspired to no other battle than riding the morning commuter to work. As that realization washed over me, so did my need to sleep.

40

Chap. 40. Lost and Found

My hunch, well, it seemed to be more than a hunch, was right. Days passed with no sign of Rickert or Chivot. Life returned to almost normal. I say almost because I still see living spirits and I'll never consider that normal. Well, would you?

For a while, at least, I could relax and focus on something else. For me, it was desperately trying to earn a living as a PI. Fortunately, Jenny was following some cases with Missing Persons, and she hired me to help her out. This provided some distraction from worry about death threats by evil spirits.

The first case was about a husband who had left the house after an argument and drove off to wherever to cool off. Although rare, he had done this several times before. Usually, he was back and cooled out within an hour or two. This time, he didn't come back. The wife filed a missing person's report and Jenny got the file.

Missing Persons cases like this one often took some time to solve and sometimes could remain open until the calendar closed them. If you planned well, you could still disappear and not be found. This wasn't one of those.

Over the next few days, Jenny and I scanned the area surrounding the missing husband's home. I was looking for green light and hoping not to see it. I didn't. Jenny and I continued to drive further, wracking our brains as to where we might find our man.

Our drive was random, and we found ourselves on the highway edging the lake. As we approached a scenic lookout at a place where high cliffs rose above the lake, I glimpsed a faint green glow. "Pull in here, I see something."

"You coulda given me a little heads up," said Jenny through her clenched teeth as she wheeled the car, tires screeching across the highway and into the small parking lot. Except for us and one other car, the place was empty. I got out to make my way to the green glow coming from the bottom of the cliff when I noticed someone sitting on the edge, staring off into space. I walked over to him. "Someone fell. He stepped around the railing and the ground gave out and he fell. I tried to call for help, but my phone doesn't work. You have to help him."

I leaned past him to look down to the lake below. There was someone down there on the rocks. From here, the way the body was laying, it must have fallen and hit the rocks below hard. I signaled for Jenny to come over. She stepped to the edge and looked over. "That doesn't look good," she said.

"You have to help him," said the man sitting on the lip of the cliff, "I think he's badly hurt."

"Don't worry," I said, "we'll look after him."

"Who you talking to," asked Jenny, looking around her, then adding, "Oh no, have we found him?"

"I think so. I asked his name."

Jenny heard his answer. It was the name on the Missing Persons file. "I guess that takes care of it. I'll call the coroner."

"The coroner," exclaimed the sitting man, "you think he's dead." He paused for a moment. "I guess he is. He was so clumsy, not paying attention, and standing too close to the edge. I suppose I should go."

He stood up and gazed blankly at me. "But, where am I going? I can't remember."

"It's ok," I said, "you'll figure it out."

"Hey," he blurted, a look of surprise on his face. "That guy down there is me. Tell my wife I'm sorry," and he vanished.

"An accident," I asked.

"Don't really know, but that's how I'll write it up. Part of the overhang seems to be broken off here. It's better for everyone."

We waited till the coroner's van arrived. Jenny spoke with them briefly and we got in the car. We would have to speak with his wife, but not until the coroner confirmed the faller's identity. Something was nagging at me, so I went ahead and said it. "How are the coroner's people going to get the body from the foot of the cliff?"

"I leave that to them. I'm sure they have their ways," was her cryptic response, then she laughed, "Let's go get a coffee."

The result of the investigation was not a happy one, but it sure beat waiting around for Rickert to come calling.

Jenny got assigned the second case shortly after wrapping up the first one. The time frame for this one was crucial. A girl of four had disappeared in a large local conservation area. As the father, who was walking with her said, "One moment she was there with me, then she wasn't."

Apparently, the girl had spotted something colorful in some thick brush, asked her dad if she could go look, but was told, no. The sight of a hawk turning circles in the sky overhead momentarily distracted the dad, and when he looked back, the

179

little girl, Nancy, was nowhere to be found. After a frantic search turning up nothing, he called the park office, who called the police.

While a search team was being assembled, Jenny and I arrived. Before joining the team, we decided to look around on or own. Like in the classic line from the movie, Taken, we had certain skills, no one else need know about, and we would find her. At least we hoped so.

The bush in the woodlot was thick and fell of brambles. Part of the conservation area's mandate was to maintain the forest in as natural a state as possible. If natural meant virtually impenetrable, filled with nasty insects and all kinds of things that could stick you, or scratch you, or take out an eye, then park service had more than achieved the goal.

We were deep in the thicket, swatting flies and pulling brambles from our clothes, when Jenny tapped me on the shoulder. "What's that," she asked, pointing to her right.

It took me several moments to locate where she was pointing, then I saw it, too. A dim, pale pink aura. We made our way towards it and discovered a shivering and fly bitten little girl in a small ditch covered with a downed tree and brush. She was asleep. Jenny bent down close to her and whispered, "Nancy."

The little girl looked up at her. "Are you an angel," she asked.

Jenny explained she was a police officer looking for a lost little girl. "Did you find her," asked the girl.

"I believe I did," smiled Jenny and reached out and lifted her into her arms.

Soon Nancy was back with her mother and father at the park office. She gave Jenny a small wave as we started back to the car. Another case solved. This one was a happy one.

Meanwhile, Vicky and Donny, the paranormal activities investigators, were gleefully following up email and phone messages about possibly haunted locations around the city.

41

Chap. 41. Goodbye and Good Luck

Thoughts of Rickert and Chivot's threat were never far from my mind but working with Jenny and apartment hunting in the city allowed me breaks from my worry. Before I had reduced him, Rickert was growing powerful, and now Chivot was with him. It meant my colleagues and I were in for a two-pronged attack. Could things get any worse? Could they ever.

I was apartment searching in one of the older parts of the city. For one reason or another, the places I visited that day weren't matching my dreams. Some were too tacky, some too expensive, and some just didn't feel right and there was one I could swear was haunted, but I didn't find any spirits there.

It had been a long day, and I was hot and exhausted. Except for that one place, living spirits were the furthest thing from my mind. Rickert and Chivot were totally out of my thoughts. I was thirsty, so I pulled into a small strip mall I was passing to buy something to drink. I pulled up in front of a small variety shop. When I got out of the car, I could hardly believe my eyes. Right next door was Kwick Optometry. Why hadn't I noticed it before?

There was Doc Dabra himself, standing at the open door. He

waved, calling me to come over. "Doc," I said as I approached him, "What are you doing here?"

"What is anyone doing here," he intoned mysteriously as he put his hand on my shoulder and guided me through the door.

His receptionist assistant was standing behind the counter. She smiled at me as I entered. "Why hello, Mr. Bannon, so nice to see you again. I trust you are well."

I still didn't know her name, so I nodded and smiled back. "Yes, thank you," was all I could say.

Doc Dabra ushered me into, a term I use loosely, his examination room and had me sit on the old dentist's chair. "So," he began, "seems you've had some success against Rickert, but are feeling some concern. Tell me what the problem is."

He sat quietly, his head tilted to one side as I told him about the encounter in the park and the battle we waged there. Then I explained about Chivot and what he told me.

After the story was done, he shook his head. "From all you've told me, you have a legitimate concern. You and your team did well to defeat him at the park. Reducing him to a small spinning ball is quite an admirable result, however, your Brother Chivot is correct. He will eventually regenerate. It will take some time, but unfortunately when he comes back, he will be more powerful than ever, and if he can merge with Chivot into a willing living body, it will increase his ability and strength even more."

"Your team is powerful, but even if you could best him in battle once again, he will come back. Living spirits can't be extinguished. There is only one way to rid the world of Rickert and Chivot and that is to send them into a different dimension, one where they can do no harm and one they can't return from. I can help you with that."

"Doc," I begged, "take these powers away from me. Send

me back to a normal life, one where living spirits are invisible, where my only worry is my daily commute and whether any woman would ever go out with me."

"You are right to be afraid, Brendan, Rickert and Chivot represent a terrible malevolence and even with them gone, the gateway to this kind of evil has been opened. I don't control your powers. They were always there, like a TV on an empty channel. I Just helped you change channels."

"But why?" I moaned, "Why did you do that. I was happy in my mundane life."

"I doubt you would find your life without attaining your true self would be very satisfying. More importantly, your world was on the verge of an unnatural infestation of evil and it was you who had the gift to fight it. This part of the world needed you."

"You mean there are others like me?"

"Around the world? A few and a few more like Detective Wenstead and your PAI pair. Without you, they would be aware of the evil, but helpless to do anything about it. They need you, the most powerful and clear-sighted one, to lead them."

"You're telling me need to accept who I am."

"No, I 'm telling you to grow into who you'll be."

That was obscure, and like everything else in my life since we first met, scary. His tone was far more businesslike. "Put your index and second fingers into those divots on the desk."

I could see two neatly cut indentations on the desktop, one for the right hand and one for the left. I obeyed Doc and placed my two index and second fingers into the indentations. The moment I did, the pain in my fingertips was excruciating. It was as if the tips of all four fingers were being ripped off, but before I could pull my hands back or scream, there was no more pain. My fingers felt normal. "What the hell was that?" I shouted, totally dismayed.

"You now have a subtle tool at your command. When you need to, you can literally slice a doorway into another dimension where you can put malevolent spirits. Since there is no return... Voila!"

Voila? What was that? He sounded like a cheesy magician who just pulled a stuffed rabbit out of his hat. He stepped to the door and signaled for me to follow. The nameless receptionist smiled as we stepped back in the storefront. "Brendan," said Doc, "would you let Isolde place her hands on your head?"

Isolde! Now, at last, I knew her name, and since it seemed I always followed Doc's suggestions, I stepped over to her. She placed her hands on the side of my head and braced myself for the pain. Nothing, just a slight tingle. Then she kissed me on the forehead and took her hands away. I could see kindness in her eyes and a warm smile lit up her face as she spoke in a gentle voice, "Goodbye and good luck, Mr. Bannon."

"Thank you, Miss Isolde," I replied.

She giggled, "Miss Isolde, so sweet!"

Doc then walked me to the door out. He opened it and reached out his hand to shake mine. I took his hand and felt the same slight tingle I had felt from Isolde's hands. "Well, Brendan," he said, "this is goodbye."

"Goodbye," I started, "What do you mean goodbye?"

"We won't be seeing each other again."

I stared in disbelief. "We won't?"

"No, it's time for Isolde and me to go. You and Detective Wenstead have all you need to lead. Oh, and don't worry, we'll find Detective Sergeant Wenstead and say goodbye."

Not feeling so good, I dragged my way to the car. How could we possibly handle all this on our own? I turned back toward him. To my utter amazement, as my mother would say, he was nowhere to be seen. Not just Doc, but Kwick Optometry, too.

There was nothing there but a closed down shop with yellowing paper taped to the windows. A seagull with a partly eaten sandwich in its beak was standing where Doc Dabra had been. It glanced up at me with an accusatory glare, got a better grip on the piece of sandwich, and flew off. My confidence and joy were like the seagull, flown. I couldn't shake the cloud of doom hanging over me on my drive home.

42

Chap. 42 New Structure

When I got home, I found out Jenny had left me a message. "Can't talk now," she said, "but I'm off for the rest of the week. Can we meet for coffee tomorrow around eleven?"

The message was cryptic, but from it, I was certain she had talked to Doc Dabra and Isolde.

I went to bed with an overwhelming sense of foreboding and although I slept, it was still there when I awoke. It was a dark cloud surrounding me as I got into the car and set off for the city and the meeting with Jenny. The bright sunlight and mild air did nothing to assuage the feeling. When I met up with Jenny in the coffee shop, I was about to tell her we were in trouble, but she beat me to the punch. "Doc Dabra and his associate...."

"Isolde."

"Ok, Isolde, have left, never to return. Without their support, we are in big trouble, Brendan."

I certainly would not tell her Doc implied it was up to us to carry on. First of all, I didn't know what that meant. There was no way I would jump around the country in an Optometry storefront and even a glimmer of the possibility of a contented Jenny, in some obscure college sweatshirt, her lovely face wreathed with steel gray locks, jumping with me was ridiculous. I returned from the disturbing image to hear Jenny saying, "Rickert is giving us a break from his attacks, but eventually, he will be back meaner and more powerful than ever if Doc Dabra is to be believed. What's more, if his ally, whatshisname..."

"Chivot," I'm the name filler inner.

"Chivot, pairs up with him, who knows what they could do."

It was a scary thought, and one I didn't wish to dwell on. "Doc Dabra also said that together we could stand against anything."

"Did he really say that?"

"Well, not exactly."

"What exactly did he say then?"

"It was a little rhyme. He said a little rhyme that you and I had everything we need to lead."

"Frankly, Brendan, I think it's going to take more than a piece of tawdry doggerel for us to stand up to Rickert, Chivot and their allies."

"You did English in college," I blurted. It was inappropriate at the moment, but I couldn't stop myself.

"Everyone does English in college, Brendan, it's mandatory. Right now, however, what's mandatory is for us to figure out what to do about Rickert and Chivot when we won't have any help from Doc Dabra."

For the next while, we banged our heads together to come up with some idea of how we might deal with the powerful living spirit of Jerry Rickert, but in the end we got nowhere. We briefly discussed Isolde's hands on our heads. "Did you get anything from her," I asked.

"Doc Dabra did something to the palms of my hands. Hurt like hell, but from her, only a slight tingle," she said.

"You can probably shoot lightning or whatever it is from your hands. But, regarding Isolde, I meant did she give you any power or knowledge? Did she give you anything?"

"Nothing I can think of except the tingle. You?"

"Same."

Whatever was intended by Isolde's laying on of hands, it didn't seem to take. The feeling of doom got way more pervasive. Jenny was correct, of course, Rickert wasn't Doc Dabra. He hadn't left forever and when he returned, he wouldn't be thinking, "Let's leave those guys alone."

At the moment, however, there was nothing more we could do but wait for Rickert's return and hope for the best. In the meantime, the best we could do is look for distractions. When Jenny was back at work, we investigated some cold cases. While they took or mind off our worries about Rickert, they didn't amount to much.

We only tracked down one missing person, and she wasn't missing at all. She had left a jealous and abusive husband who had filed the missing person's report hoping to find her and exact revenge. Eight years later, she was a blackjack dealer at a distant casino and a contented member of the LGBT community. The case was closed without informing the husband, who was unlikely to care at this point. After seven years, he had gotten an annulment and had remarried.

Meanwhile, Vicky and Danny, the paranormal activity inves-tigators, were following up on emails and phone calls about haunted buildings and eerie events. They got some material for their TV program, but most of the messages they received didn't lead to much.

Whenever they found something promising, they would often call Jenny or me to confirm the viability of what they sensed about the location. On rare occasions, when they felt over-whelmed by a place, they would ask me to come by and check it out with them. I have to tell you that true hauntings are almost nonexistent.

Living spirits weren't ghosts and in the most cases were in transition from this world to wherever they go. Those who stayed around for any length of time did so for reasons similar to Fitz, or Lisa Durban, or Steel. For the most part, they were looking for a proper final resting place for their earthly remains, or in other cases, like Ken, they didn't know they were dead. A minuscule number kept an attachment to someone or something and deliberately hung around.

Chivot was one of these until he encountered Rickert who, as Doc Dabra explained, was one of a handful of truly evil spirits intent on manipulating and using the living for whatever was their nefarious purpose. Destroying me, for example.

Most of the places I visited with Vicky and Dan tended to be disappointing for them but delighted me. I didn't want to see signs of haunting. Leaky radiators, cold sensitive building materials, undetected gaps in the walls, or an odd play of lights from neighboring street lighting meant the places were not haunted. It was something I truly appreciated. I didn't want to encounter any living spirit for fear word would get back to Rickert and exacerbate his murderous intentions regarding me. Fitz was spirit enough.

Until the fateful day when they called to tell me about a place they were going to visit. They had received several emails convincing them that this place showed clear signs of paranormal activity and they should check it out. One email, they told me, suggested they bring fellow investigators because there was so much going on for them to deal with. The place these emails suggested an impressed Vicky was a deserted commune called The New Structure.

The New Structure commune! I sensed my panic rising as I shouted, "Don't go near there. Stay away, it's a dangerous place."

I was having trouble controlling an overwhelming sense of trepidation about New Structure. That was Chivot's place.

"Don't go there." I croaked.

"Too late," giggled Vicky, "we're already here. See you soon."

"No," I cried as her phone turned off.

43

Chap. 43. Ready to Burn

The instant Vicky's call ended, I was on the phone to Jenny. She barely had time to say hello when I started shouting into the phone, my words tripping all over each other. "We gotta go save David and Vicky. New Structure is where Chivot hangs out. Rickert is likely there. Oh, are you off duty? We have to help them. They're in big trouble."

As I took a deep breath, Jenny broke in, her tone flippant, "Great to talk with you, Brendan. Now, if you don't mind, could you take a moment to calmly explain what you were hollering about?"

I paused, gathered my thoughts, and spoke again. This time, my voice was calmer and steady. "I just got a call from Vicky. She and Don got some emails suggesting they visit the old New Structure commune because there was lots of mysterious stuff going on there. She called to tell me the two of them had just arrived and I... we, should join them."

"And why would that be? I just shed my uni, it was a long week, lots of meetings over at district and I'm exhausted."

"New Structure is Chivot's place. I think he or Rickert found a way to send those emails. Vicky and Donny are walking into huge trouble."

"So, I sense you believe it's a setup to get us there, too? What if we don't go? I don't like the idea of walking into a trap."

"Me either, but Vicky and Donny don't stand a chance without us."

"Alright," Jenny sighed, "tell me how to get there."

I gave her the directions as I sprinted to my car. Moments later, I was on the road heading for who knows what. Nothing good, that was for sure. I spent most of the trip trying to figure out what we could do. It had taken everything we had to beat Rickert last time. Now he would be much more powerful, and probably merged his powers with Chivot's. And as far as I'm concerned, Doc Dabra left me high and dry. The sense of doom that dogged me earlier flooded back with a vengeance. I wanted to run in the opposite direction, but I couldn't leave Vicky and Donny at the mercy of those evil spirits.

On one hand, it seemed like forever and on the other, only a couple of minutes when the overgrown signpost for the New Structures commune appeared ahead, I turned in, making my way up the long drive, past the farmhouse, where I first encountered a living spirit, to the parking lot of the large meeting hall. The Paranormal Activities van was parked in front. Two dark colored half ton trucks stood as silent escorts, one to either side.

As I pulled up beside the nearest truck, I could see Jenny's car in the rear-view mirror pulling in behind me. Getting out, I stood by the driver's door until she joined me. Together we hurried towards the brightly painted doors of the meeting hall. "Somebody has been looking after this place," whispered Jenny, as I yanked open the door.

Inside, the meeting hall was well lit. I could see several balloons hanging from the roof beneath lit candles. Two of them were right above the heads of Donny and Vicky, who were seated side by side on a pew. They sat rigidly facing straight ahead towards a small stage centered with an ornate podium. I called their names, but neither one turned to look my way. It was as if they were frozen in place. Jenny stepped beside me just as Chivot spoke. "Detective Wenstead, Brendan, welcome to my humble abode. How do you like it, it's exactly the way it looked so many years ago when the community gathered to send off our spirits? Apparently, the rest of the members weren't so eager to leave. My son, Everett, has taken excellent care of it. I sent him away that day with instructions to keep up the meeting hall in memory of the commune members who moved to glory from there. As it turned out, it was only me. No matter, I shall gather them all in the days ahead."

"As I'm sure you noticed when you came in, there are those very interesting decorations hanging from the ceiling. May I draw you attention to the ones above your two paranormal activities cable TV stars? They, like all the others, consist of balloons filled with an extremely incendiary liquid. Above each, you can see a flame. They are quite lovely, don't you think? Can you believe it, sheer will power holds them up? As I am speaking to you, I am using psychic magnetism, Rickert's term, elegant, isn't it, to prevent them from falling. Should anything happen to me, they will instantly fall. The balloons will burst open and the accelerant they contain will be ignited by the flame, causing an extremely hot fire everywhere, but especially on the heads of your two friends. Just a word to the wise. Oh, and by the way, they cannot move on their own. Brother Rickert and I have seen to that."

Jenny leaned over, poking me with her elbow as she whispered, "This guy, and all I can see of him is a wavering in the air, is chattier than you are."

I turned towards her, whispering my response, "I become a blabbermouth when I'm anxious or afraid. He's crowing. Are you impressed?"

"What, at the freshly varnished walls, or the fireballs hanging from nothing over Vicky and Donny's heads or the gabby invisible man? Where the hell is this going, anyway? Get on with it," she shouted.

This was a different Jenny. It was neither the cop, nor the hot young lady. This was something stronger, more in control. I liked it, but I wasn't sure how smart it was to challenge what we knew to be two powerful evil spirits.

We didn't have long to wait. A large, middle-aged man wearing overalls and a plaid shirt stepped out from the shadows. A strong red and black aura enveloped him. "Rickert!" exclaimed Jenny.

Chivot spoke, "I will join him momentarily, but before I do, let me introduce my son, Everett. He is willingly cooperating with Brother Rickert and myself."

He stepped toward the one he called Everett, the one possessed by Rickert and to my amazement Chivot seemed to merge with him. An orange and gray flame mingled with the red and black of Rickert's aura. In that instant, a wave of pulsating energy engulfed us. The impact sent me reeling backward. The pain that came with the impact, was as if someone had thrown scalding hot water all over me. I could hear Jenny groan. The struggle to look over to see if she was alright was too difficult. The scalding water had turned to a burning acid.

Despite the pain, both Jenny and I raised our hands in response, the bluish green lightning from mine blending with a stream of golden light from Jenny's. Everett stumbled backward. I don't think his possessors expected this. I know I didn't. For a second, the pain vanished, then was back again as a second wave of energy struck.

44

Chap. 44. Battle and Wakening

Like the battle in the park, this was the oddest form of warfare one could possibly imagine. To an informed spectator, it would look like nothing more than some sort of standoff, amounting to nothing. For the participants, at least on our side, it was a matter of life and death. Unseen, but deadly, waves of energy pulsed across the space between us. The lightning from Jenny and my hands countering the forces from Everett and the two evil spirits who possessed him. Red and black, orange and gray waves intensified and faded around him in the back and forth.

I felt unexpectedly strong and confident. Out of the corner of my eye, I saw an intense and persistent golden bolt of bright energy. It told me she felt the same. Between the two of us, we seemed to carry the fight to them. The auras surrounding Chivot's son seemed to fade, pulling back. I was thinking we had them on the run, we would soon wear them down to tiny whirling balls we could safely deal with; then send them to an empty universe. Then something changed.

The auras surrounding Everett seemed to swiftly spread out in every direction, blazing like a burst of celebratory fireworks only a hundred times brighter. For a moment, I thought the brightness had affected my eyes, as a dark haze seemed to reach out from those flames. As it did, it grew solider. I saw a pair of flaring orange eyes peering at me as the darkening cloud grew into a hideous figure. Orange flaming eyes surrounded by a rat-like face. Enormous bat-like wings stretching out, reaching to engulf us. It was a terrible and a terrifying sight and I knew it was real.

This creature, whatever it was, was clearly a construct of a deadly evil and it was about to consume Jenny and me; suck us in to a vile emptiness. Overwhelmed by dread, I closed my eyes, awaiting the incomprehensible horror of the cruel maw. I couldn't watch as it reached out to consume me. "No," cried Jenny.

The moment I closed my eyes, I felt myself step away from the fight. I was no longer in the New Structure meeting room. Although I was on some level aware the battle with Rickert and Chivot continued, I sensed I was alone in a dark and empty space. Had the evil entity emanating from Rickert and Chivot ingested me? I looked around for Jenny but could see no sign of her.

The absolute darkness was strangely soothing. For a brief moment, I wondered if I was dead, then realized I still sensed myself engaged in the odd battle of conflicting energies. My body was wracked with pain, but it seemed so far away. In that instant, the darkness engulfing me was ripped apart by what looked like a giant Omnimax screen bearing thousands of images of faces.

As I gazed in amazement, the faces seemed to grow before my eyes, manifesting themselves until I could clearly recognize their features. Many were vaguely human looking, others were hideous by earth standards, faces that would instantly engulf the viewer in horror. Yet, I didn't feel any fear. All the faces, human and nonhuman, exuded a benevolence beyond anything I had felt before.

As I watched, the multiple faces resolved themselves into one huge visage, reminding me of Doc Dabra. It wasn't him, but a composite of all the faces that had opened on the giant screen. Only thing, it wasn't two dimensional, like a movie, but had a three-dimensional quality making me believe I was literally standing in its living presence.

It spoke to me. Not in words, but in my head. The tone was gentle and reassuring. What it said without words, I heard as, "Welcome to our family Brendan of earth. You and the one who stands beside you bravely fighting in this battle join us in the never-ending war against unworldly evil rising from those corrupted members of your species like the ones with whom you are now engaged and from other evil forces drawn to your world by such as them."

"We are here for you in your need, but know you are one who is now a part of our family. As one with us in your faith and resolve, there are few who can stand against you. Be strong, believe, victory will be yours."

I opened my eyes. The shadow monster had disappeared, but the waves of energy from Rickert and Cheviot remained just as intense, the pain just as extreme. On one level, I wanted to turn and run from there with all the strength I could muster. On another level, I felt a firm resolve, a belief the world depended on me and on Jenny and we needed to push the waves of crippling pain coming at us far from our minds and dig deeper into our reserves.

The lightning from our hands increased, merging into a steady beam of gold and green. The flaming red and orange and black aura enveloping Everett would flare and then dim. When dimmed, Rickert and Chivot would take form, then the auras would flare again, and Everett stood alone.

My hands were aching, my legs trembled, pain shot up my spine as each pulse of energy from the hostile spirits struck me. I was certain Jenny felt the same. Despite the discomfort, we could easily maintain our attack. Almost indiscernibly, Everett was backing away from us. Rickert and Chivot appeared more frequently. The auras around Everett were weaker in their flaring. Jenny shouted, "Open the portal, Brendan."

At her shout, I slashed my right hand in an arc from ceiling to floor. A matching golden line appeared behind Everett, then widened, revealing what appeared to be a wall of darkness. I knew for a fact it was simply nothingness. Our attack intensified, and Everett continued to back off as the spirits of Rickert and Chivot became more solid. We pushed them back to the edge of the portal, but their defense was fierce. The malevolence of their attack brought me to my knees. Then, once again, I could hear the calm voice inside my head, "Be strong, believe," and my body seemed to diminish as I sent out a massive wave of something, energy, will, life force. Whatever it was, it was powerful.

Everett had backed to the edge of the portal as my force, blending with Jenny's, brought the two living spirits into focus. As they did, a form came racing across the floor, reached out and grabbed at the two spirits, carrying them through the portal into the nothingness. "Close the portal, now," came an anxious sounding shout from the emptiness.

"Fitz!"

"Now, Brendan!"

I had never heard Fitz so resolute and assured. I closed the portal, and my heart sank. Fitz had fallen into the nothingness with the two evil ones. Thanks to his sacrifice, we had won. I had no time to dwell on his loss, as Jenny grabbed my arm and pointed towards Vicky and Donny. The balloons of accelerant were falling, and tongues of flame were licking at them.

Moving as fast as we could, it took only a couple of seconds to reach the two. Jenny grabbed Vicky and pulled her to her feet as I yanked up a dazed Donny from where he sat. The four of us staggered to the door as the accelerant burst into flames around us. As we made our way to safety beyond the building, I took a backward glance to see if Everett was escaping the flames behind us, but he was nowhere to be seen.

We moved the cars away from the intensely blazing meeting hall. Jenny called 911. We waited until the fire department arrived. Although it had only taken them a short time, the meeting hall was little more than smoking rubble when they got there.

As for Everett, we later learned they found his charred body on the remains of a small cot in a back room, a glass tumbler still welded to his hands. An analysis of the contents indicated it was akin to Chivot's suicide brew. Everett was likely dead before the flames reached him.

As for me, I was already missing Fitz. I couldn't believe he was no longer here. He had become such a constant presence in my life. He was continuously helping me adjust to my bizarre and increasing abilities. It would take me a long time to get over his loss. We will never know if Jenny and I could have successfully driven Rickert and Chivot through the portal on our own, but there is little doubt his sacrifice bought us the time to rescue Vicky and Don. I just felt terrible for him, lost for eternity in a dimension of nothingness with the likes of Rickert and Chivot.

45

Chap. 45. Aftermath

According to several veteran firefighters, they had never seen anything like the fire at the New Structure's meeting house. It had burned so quickly and so cleanly. It was so focused in its destructiveness it had not even scorched the nearby fence and trees. They said it was a miracle, a fire that burned as ferociously as it did, had remained so confined and so complete. Virtually nothing of the building remained, not even the floor.

Oddly enough, the staging room where Everett Chivot's body was found, although decimated like the rest of the meeting house, had left the pallet and body only partially burned. As one firefighter said, "the arsonists were experts."

What he would never know was just how painstaking those arsonists were or the reason. Their plan had been to leave no recognizable trace of either Jenny, me, or our two associate paranormal activity investigators. The actual miracle was not the swiftness and ferocity of the fire, but the fact all four of us had escaped it.

Vicky and Donny were in no condition to drive. They were both still traumatized by the events of their day. The mysterious forces binding them to chairs under tongues of flame over containers of fire accelerant. The state they were in allowed them to perceive just enough of what was happening and know what was planned for them. No surprise, even after the fire was nothing more than burning coals, they were still nearly comatose.

Jenny arranged with the local police officer following up on the fire call to leave the Paranormal Activity Investigations van in the parking lot overnight. It was OK, as long as it wasn't in the way of fire trucks or arson investigators. They believed Everett had died in the fire, so they would be taking a closer look.

Since I lived in the opposite direction, Jenny would drive them. Vicky, who was still quite shaken, but far more aware than Donny, said it would be fine if Jenny took them to the cable office and they could find their way home from there. When Jenny doubled down on the offer to drive them to their house, Vicky explained they didn't live together. Her sister would close the office soon and could take her home, and Donny's boyfriend could come and get him.

Donny's boyfriend? Well, there you go. You learn something new every day. All along, I thought Vicky and Donny were an item. So, I might see a lot of things most people don't see, but recognizing some things most other people see, not so much. When Jenny agreed to take them to the cable company offices, Vicky was alert enough to get some of the more valuable pieces from the van, a camera and sound equipment. She shoved them into the trunk of Jenny's car, and then, with Jenny's help, put the still dazed Donny into the back seat.

Moments later, they pulled out of the parking lot and were off. I got into my car and headed for home. The first thing I did pulling out on the highway was what I often did, Ask Fitz what

203

was next. Only this time, Fitz had no answer. Fitz was gone, and he wasn't coming back. I felt terrible. For the rest of the way home, my thoughts ran from Fitz, lost in an empty universe with no one for company but Rickert and Chivot. Neither one of whom would be thrilled with him.

Then, my mind wandered back to the faces that had appeared to me during the battle. The ones welcoming me to the ranks of intergalactic, inter universe, fighters of supernatural evil. Like the Winchesters, only with lots of extraterrestrial allies. I got some distraction from the many concerns my new role would mean as well as losing my spectral friend Fitz by trying to decide if I was Dean or Sam. Other than the supernatural thing, we had nothing in common.

Dumb as it was, it got me home without freaking out over what had gone down not so much earlier and getting into an accident. No, it kept me going till I got through the door of my apartment and then I freaked out. I shouted and threw stuff around the living room until one of my neighbors knocked on the wall. With that, I grabbed a beer from the fridge, sat down in front of the tv, turned it on, and promptly fell asleep.

Next morning, while I was sweeping up the broken pieces of glass from the cup I tossed and the lamp I sent flying, the phone rang. It was Jenny, and she was as intense as I had ever heard her, even in her full-blown, official investigation mode. She wanted to see me and right away. I got the message and minutes later was in the car, heading down the highway to the city.

We met up where we always did in the coffee shop near my former place of work. I had just chosen a corner table and set down the two lattes I bought when she came through the door. Her expression wasn't one of delight. It was as if a storm cloud was hanging over her head as she briskly pushed back the chair and sat. Leaning over the table, she glanced at the latte and muttered, "Thanks."

Then the words seemed to fly out of her mouth. "I like my job. I enjoy what I'm doing. It's important to me."

I wasn't sure where that came from, but whatever was on her mind, I wasn't going to interrupt. "All my life," she continued, "I wanted to be a member of the police. I'm not giving it up!"

"OK," I said, but she wasn't listening.

She had more, adding, "I want to continue being a police officer. There is no way in hell I'm going to be Isolde, the receptionist, to your Doc Dabra. I don't care what magic powers she has. You will not talk me into hopping around the continent in a grubby old storefront chasing evil spirits and smiling for the potential spook spotters you might be wakening."

I got the picture. She was basically expressing my own thoughts, except for the full-time job and the Isolde thing. "I don't want it either," I emphasized, then added, "I assume you're telling me this because you had a visit from the other-world folk during our fight with Rickert and Chivot, too."

Jenny sounded calmer, saying, "I did and yeah, I know it's important, and I sort of agreed to join you in fighting the evil those two spirits represented. In a way, it is a police job, but I don't want to give up what I already have."

"Well," I said, trying to sound reasonable, "there can't be too many evil spirits or whatever around and to tell the truth the idea of hopping around the continent in a grubby old shop is not something that appeals to me either. So, you keep your police job and I'll continue being a private eye who supplements his income as a freelance copywriter. Deal?"

"Deal."

She smiled and sipped at her latte. Afterwards, we took a walk along the street towards my former workplace. We passed the spot where the taxi hit and killed Ken, and the fancy new building overlaying the site where I first met Fitz. We said little as we walked along, but I guess we both knew there was a special bond linking us. Neither of us knew what it might mean down the road, but for now things were cool.

46

Chap. 46. The Phone Rang

After that, life went back to normal. At least as normal as it can be for people like us, destined to seek out and save the world from heaven knows what evil we might encounter down the road. Jenny was occupied with her job and Vicky's and Donny's Paranormal Activities Investigations cable show was an unexpected success, finding its way on to one of the major cable networks. As for me, I spent more time as a freelance writer than a private eye, although the PI work I took on, along with my writing, provided me with a pretty good income.

I moved to the city, getting an apartment close to Jenny and the cable television offices. We would meet occasionally to share information and, as we got to know each other better, to enjoy each other's company. As for the evil, what any of us came across was nothing more than the mundane evil of human foibles. We were all slipping into a pleasant complacency until the night the ringing of the phone awakened me from my sleep.

www.ingramcontent.com/pod-product-compliance
Lightning Source LLC
Chambersburg PA
CBHW051250250626
47155CB00009B/3238